A HARP
A SLING
A CAVE
And
A CROWN
THE LIFE OF KING DAVID

Steve E. Upchurch

A Harp, A Sling, A Cave and A Crown: The Life of King David
Author: Steve E. Upchurch
Copyright ©2024 Steve E. Upchurch
Cover Design: Crystal Deeds Cover Photo: Steve Upchurch
Layout and Editing by Crystal Deeds
Set in Academy Engraved LET Plain, Calibri
Printed in the United States

Books may be ordered online at: Amazon.com and BarnesandNoble.com, through: Steve E. Upchurch's Facebook page: by direct communication with the Author by email at Steveup93@hotmail.com or by phone 618.780.7564.

The views of this book are solely the views of Steve E. Upchurch. The stories in this book are written from the imagined first person perspective of the historical, biblical narrative of King David and are based on the Biblical texts found in First and Second Samuel and First Kings. The main characters in this book are based on the factual, historical characters in the Holy Bible, however, the author has taken the liberty of artistic expression.

ISBN: 978-1-7377786-5-3 (Paperback edition)

ISBN: 978-1-7377786-3-9 (ePub edition)

ISBN: 978-1-7377786-4-6 (Kindle edition)

All scripture references are taken from the Holy Bible, King James Version and the New International Version®, NIV® Copyright ©1973, 1978, 1984, 2011 by Biblica, Inc.® Used by permission. All rights reserved worldwide.

(Please note, some verses are paraphrased within the context of the narrative of the characters within this story but remain true to the main facts in the Bible.)

INTRODUCTION

The story of David is intricate because David himself was a complex man. His life was marked by both conflict and joy, pain and blessing, suffering and favor from God. He experienced overwhelming success and public adulation, yet he also faced profound failure and betrayal. He was celebrated with parades and songs about his military victories, only to see a significant portion of the nation turn against him, including betrayal by two of his own sons. His greatest adversary was the previous king, while his closest friend was that same king's very own son.

David witnessed his son Solomon rise to greatness and renown, while another son, Absalom, is remembered as a traitor. Despite his strong faith and trust in God, David struggled with his weaknesses, particularly with beautiful women. He was a formidable leader in battle but faltered as a father and husband. Armed with a harp and a sling, he navigated many trials while ultimately finding himself on the throne wearing a crown.

Throughout these challenges, David maintained his relationship with God and earned the title *"a man after God's own heart"* (1 Samuel 13:14 / Acts 13:22).

His battle with Goliath set a timeless standard for the underdog, and the phrase "David versus Goliath" resonates through the ages. With his harp, David soothed troubled spirits and composed worship songs, while his sword made him a powerful and ruthless warrior. Michelangelo's statue of David, standing seventeen feet tall, is one of the world's most renowned works of art. Countless songs have been inspired by the psalms David wrote, and his twenty-third psalm is among the most famous chapters in the Bible.

David is mentioned at least fifty times in the New Testament. The first verse in the gospels introduces Jesus as "the son of David, the son of Abraham." Joseph, Jesus' earthly father, is referred to as "the son of David" by the angel who announced the conception of Jesus. Jesus himself referenced David when discussing the Sabbath and was often called "Lord, Son of David" by those seeking healing or deliverance. In the book of Acts, David is frequently cited, from Peter's mention of David's prophecy regarding Judas to quotes from David being used in sermons. Paul also references David in his letters to the Romans and Timothy. And in the book of Revelation David is mentioned three times, with Jesus declaring Himself as *"the Root and the Offspring of David"* (Revelation 22:16).

Among Old Testament figures like Moses, Joshua, Elijah, and Elisha, it was David's name chosen for Jerusalem, making it "The City of David." He is the one and only David in the Bible.

David remains a beacon of light and hope for those who have suffered major, temporary, moral failures or have fallen spiritually. His prayer of repentance in Psalm 51 is the model prayer for anyone that is seeking restoration with the Lord.

THE BEGINNING

A lone. Ignored. Invisible. That is how I felt.

My name is David. I am the youngest of eight sons born to my father, Jesse. (1 Sam. 16:10-11 & 1 Sam. 17:12-14 NIV) I grew up in the hill country near Bethlehem. My earliest memories revolve around music. My mother, Nitzevet, would rock me in her arms while singing ancient Jewish songs that had been passed down through the generations, such as the songs of Moses and Deborah.

I was raised in a rich heritage, surrounded by tales of our ancestors, songs of victory and triumph, and praise to Jehovah God. One song my mother sang frequently was the victory song written by Moses after God parted the Red Sea. The repetition of this song and its thrilling story shaped my dreams and aspirations, inspiring many of the psalms I would later write:

> The Song of Moses:
> "I will sing to the Lord, for He is highly exalted.
> Both horse and driver He has hurled into the sea.
>
> "The Lord is my strength and my defense; He has become my salvation.
> He is my God, and I will praise Him, my father's God, and I will exalt Him.
> The Lord is a warrior; the Lord is His name.
> Pharaoh's chariots and his army He has hurled into the sea.
> The best of Pharaoh's officers are drowned in the Red Sea.
> The deep waters have covered them; they sank to the depths like a stone.
> Your right hand, Lord, was majestic in power.
> Your right hand, Lord, shattered the enemy.

"In the greatness of Your majesty You threw down those who opposed You.
You unleashed Your burning anger; it consumed them like stubble.
By the blast of Your nostrils the waters piled up.
The surging waters stood up like a wall; the deep waters congealed in the heart of the sea.
The enemy boasted, 'I will pursue, I will overtake them.
I will divide the spoils; I will gorge myself on them.
I will draw my sword and my hand will destroy them.'
But You blew with Your breath, and the sea covered them.
They sank like lead in the mighty waters.
Who among the gods is like You, Lord?
Who is like You—majestic in holiness, awesome in glory, working wonders?

"You stretch out Your right hand, and the earth swallows Your enemies.
In Your unfailing love You will lead the people You have redeemed.
In Your strength You will guide them to Your holy dwelling.
The nations will hear and tremble; anguish will grip the people of Philistia.
The chiefs of Edom will be terrified, the leaders of Moab will be seized with trembling, the people of Canaan will melt away; terror and dread will fall on them.
By the power of Your arm they will be as still as a stone—until Your people pass by, Lord, until the people You bought pass by.
You will bring them in and plant them on the mountain of Your inheritance—the place, Lord, You made for Your dwelling, the sanctuary, Lord, Your hands established.

"The Lord reigns for ever and ever." (Exodus 15:1-18 NIV)

This song illustrated how words set to music could vividly portray hope and inspiration. Often, I would daydream about witnessing the waters part and the Israelites walking through on dry ground. I imagined touching the wall of water and seeing fish swimming by, as if puzzled by the sight of people walking underwater! I pictured myself as part of the choir singing triumphantly as the bodies of Egyptian soldiers floated to the surface.

Little did I realize that the words of Moses' song, which I learned as a child, would chart the course of my life. The passion stirred by these words fueled my desire to write similar heartfelt psalms that would glorify the Lord.

As I grew into a teenager, I enjoyed spending time with my older brothers, listening to their stories of hunting and adventure. However, they often saw me as a nuisance, asking too many questions and getting in their way. I found myself blending into the shadows while my father and brothers shared tales of mighty men and warriors.

I loved hearing my father recount how God spoke to Abraham, promising to make his descendants as numerous as the stars. I admired the dramatic retelling of the angel halting Abraham's sacrifice of Isaac. I was captivated by the story of Joseph, who went from being thrown into a pit by his brothers to becoming second in command in Egypt.

I admit I felt a pang of jealousy as my father's favor clearly went to my oldest brother, but I enjoyed imagining myself at the Battle of Jericho, playing a trumpet as the walls fell. I also cherished the romance stories my mother told, particularly about Rahab the Harlot, who helped the spies in Jericho and ended up as my great-great-grandmother. My favorite romance was the story of Boaz and Ruth, my great-grandparents. Their story fascinated me, and I loved hearing how Ruth, a Moabite princess, chose to follow Naomi instead of staying in her royal position. As I sat on her lap, little did my mother know that I would eventually become king of Israel, continuing our royal lineage and seeing Solomon, my son, become king as well.

THE ANOINTING

Then came the day that changed my life forever. It began like any other day. I was tending the sheep when my brother, Ozem, came running, breathless from a long sprint.

"Come quickly!" he shouted, gasping for air.

"Why?" I asked, alarmed. "Is something wrong with Father? Did something happen to Mother?"

"No, nothing like that!" Ozem replied. "Samuel the prophet is in Bethlehem, where we offer sacrifices, and he wants to see you!"

"Me?" I asked, puzzled. "What could Samuel possibly want with me?"

Impatiently, Ozem gave me a shove towards Bethlehem. "Just go! I'm staying here to watch the sheep, so come back as soon as he's done with you!"

As I turned to leave, Ozem shouted after me, "I said GO! Run as fast as you can! Samuel is making everyone wait for you!"

Still bewildered, I sprinted toward the gathering. My mind raced with questions. *What could the prophet want with me? Does he have a task for me at the temple?*

When I arrived, sure enough, Ozem had been right. Everyone was standing and staring in my direction as I approached. My father rushed out to meet me, pointing towards the prophet with a stern expression.

"Go stand before Samuel," he ordered.

"What does he want?" I asked, confused.

"I don't know," he replied, impatiently. "Just do as you're told!"

Hesitantly, I stepped forward, standing before Samuel, still unsure of what was happening. No one knew it yet, but due to King Saul's disobedience, God had revealed to Samuel that He was removing His favor from Saul and was going to anoint someone from our household.

7

As Samuel squinted, peering into my face, a shiver ran down my spine. It felt like he was looking straight into my soul. Then, Samuel closed his eyes, slowly raising his hands to the heavens and stood in silence for several long moments.

I glanced nervously at my father, silently asking, *What is he doing?*

My father frowned, nodding towards Samuel as if to say, *Pay attention.*

Suddenly, Samuel shouted, "Yes, Lord!" startling everyone. His eyes locked on mine, and with an authoritative voice, he declared, "You are the one!"

I stood there, bewildered, not understanding what he meant by "the one." Samuel then took the ram's horn filled with oil from around his neck and poured it over my head, letting it flow into my hair. He didn't stop until the last drop had been used.

At first, I was embarrassed by what was happening. But as the oil ran down my neck and shoulders, I felt something extraordinary—something far beyond the oil itself. It was the Spirit of the Lord!

Warmth spread from the top of my head down my spine, tingling throughout my entire body until it reached my feet. *What was that?* I thought, awestruck. Whatever it was, I knew I never wanted it to leave me. That feeling—the Spirit—would come upon me many times throughout my life, and it changed me.

I arrived that day as a boy with no clear direction, but I left as a young man, anointed by God.

After finishing the anointing, Samuel abruptly turned and announced, "I'm off to Ramah." We all stood in stunned silence, watching him walk away, awed by what had just occurred.

Still feeling the presence of the Spirit, I turned to my father and asked, "Father, what was that all about?"

My father explained what had happened before I arrived—how Samuel had summoned him and all the elders for a sacrifice.

"What did he want?" I asked.

"He didn't say," my father replied. "He just prayed over me and your brothers, starting with Eliab. Samuel seemed impressed with him at first."

"Well, who wouldn't be?" I quipped. "Just look at him!"

My father chuckled, then continued. "Samuel just stood there looking at Eliab, but after a moment, he shook his head and mumbled something to himself."

"What was he mumbling?"

"I think he was talking to God," my father said. "Whatever it was, it appeared God told him 'No', because Samuel mumbled something about not looking at outward appearance, that the Lord looks at the heart."

My father went on, "Then Samuel said, 'The Lord has not chosen this one.' He called Abinadab next, but it was the same—'Neither has the Lord chosen this one.' Samuel went through all of your brothers, and each time, he said the same thing."

My father paused, looking at me. "So, apparently, you are the one the Lord has chosen."

"Me?" I asked, astonished.

"Seems so," my father said with a wry smile. "I'm as surprised as you are."

"So, what now?" I asked, feeling a mix of excitement and uncertainty.

My father shrugged, scratching his head. "I suppose you go back to watching the sheep."

After such a profound experience of being anointed and feeling the Spirit of the Lord, returning to the sheep felt anticlimactic. But that's exactly what I did. Little did I know, at that very moment, the Spirit of the Lord was being lifted from King Saul as it came upon me.

THE LION

It was another typical evening in Bethlehem. The sheep grazed on the lush green grass covering the long, sloping hillside just outside the town. It was early summer, and the sun was slowly setting, leaving behind a breathtaking cascade of brilliant colors.

Several weeks had passed since Samuel anointed me, and life had returned to its usual rhythm. As the youngest son, I was still tasked with watching the sheep. My father and I had spoken at length about the meaning of Samuel's actions and his declaration that I was "the one." Yet, my father was as puzzled as I was regarding what that actually meant.

"Do you think I'm going to be called to serve in the tabernacle?" I asked.

"No," my father replied. "To serve in the tabernacle, you must be from the tribe of Levi. We are from the tribe of Judah."

He paused, then lowered his voice and glanced over his shoulder as if a spy might be listening. "I wonder if you were anointed as king," he whispered. "But that can't be," he continued in a hushed tone. "Saul is still on the throne. I suppose we'll just have to wait and see what it all means," my father concluded, shaking his head in bewilderment.

Still, I couldn't push the thought from my mind. *Don't think about it,* I told myself, trying to focus on watching the sheep. *Just do what you always do.* But the questions kept swirling in my head.

As I sat there, three distinct sounds echoed down the hillside into the valley below: the soft bleating of sheep, the melodic notes of my harp, and the sound of my voice. As my singing and the harp's melody grew louder, the sheep's bleating gradually softened, comforted by the familiar sound of their shepherd's voice. I sang a song I had written:

> *"O Lord, our Lord, how excellent is Thy name in all the earth!*
> *Who hast set Thy glory above the heavens.*

Out of the mouth of babes and sucklings hast Thou ordained strength because of Thine enemies, that Thou mightest still the enemy and the avenger.

"When I consider Thy heavens, the work of Thy fingers, the moon and the stars, which Thou hast ordained; what is man, that Thou art mindful of him?
And the son of man, that Thou visitest him?
For Thou hast made him a little lower than the angels, and hast crowned him with glory and honour.

"Thou madest him to have dominion over the works of Thy hands; Thou hast put all things under his feet: All sheep and oxen, yea, and the beasts of the field; the fowl of the air, and the fish of the sea, and whatsoever passeth through the paths of the seas.

"O Lord our Lord, how excellent is Thy name in all the earth!"
(Psalm 8 KJV)

As my voice echoed down the mountain side the sheep grew quiet and settled down for the night.

Eventually, I laid the harp down, and as the night air grew cooler, I snuggled in between the warm blankets my mother had packed for me. And as I did every night, I looked up into the night sky and worshiped my Creator, softly repeating some of the words I had written…

"O Lord, our Lord, how excellent is Your name in all the earth."

Once more I felt the Spirit of the Lord near me… IN me!

Then the night sounds suddenly grew eerily silent. The frogs stopped croaking… the crickets stopped chirping…

As the hair stood up on the back of my neck, I became intensely aware of my surroundings. Chill bumps covered my arms and legs, even though my body was warm beneath the thick blanket. My breathing quickened as my heart began beating violently inside my chest… I knew what it was…

A lion!!!

Panic gripped my mind, unsure of what to do. But then, an unusual calmness filled my heart and mind as the words of my song echoed in my spirit: *Through the praise of children and infants, You have established a stronghold against Your enemies, to silence the foe and the avenger!*

To silence the foe... I knew what I had to do.

Hearing the cry of the lamb, now in the lion's mouth, a surge of adrenaline coursed through me. I threw off the blanket, leaped to my feet, and sprinted toward the sound as fast as I could. With the victory song still lingering on my lips, I ran fearlessly to where the ferocious lion stood with the helpless lamb in its jaws. Without hesitation, I jumped on the lion's back, grabbed the beast by its mane with one hand, wrapped my other arm around its jaw, and twisted with all my might! A loud crack echoed into the night as the lion's neck snapped.

I quickly pulled down on the lion's lower jaw, causing it to release the whimpering lamb into my arms. *"It's okay,"* I whispered to the trembling lamb. *"You're safe now, in the arms of your shepherd."*

As I walked back to my campsite, I looked up at the starry night and thought about the Great Shepherd and how He cares for us, His sheep. By the light of the campfire, I gently cleaned the lamb's wounds, applied ointment and healing oil from my shepherd's bag, all the while giving thanks to Almighty God for giving me the strength to do the impossible.

When I finally settled back beneath my blanket, with the injured lamb snuggled against me, I lay there thinking, *Where did that come from? What just happened?* I knew that what had transpired was not by my might, but because of the Spirit of the Lord that was with me!

Over the next few days, I carried the injured lamb on my shoulders as I tended to the other sheep, singing a song of comfort. Little did I know the significance of what I had just learned through this experience and how the Lord was preparing me for the battles I would face in the future.

THE BEAR

S *urely that's not what I think it is...* I thought to myself.

But it was—a bear!

First a lion, and now a bear? And not just any bear—this was a Syrian Brown Bear.

And she was huge, easily five hundred pounds! Worse, she had a small lamb clamped between her jaws.

I knew immediately it was too late to save the lamb. But I also knew that once a bear developed a taste for lamb, it would surely return for more.

Once again, I felt the calming presence of the Lord wash over me. I felt prompted to reach into my shepherd's bag and pull out my sling. But I hesitated. *A sling and a stone against a Syrian Brown Bear?*

I had become quite accurate at hitting practice targets, but this was something entirely different. *What if I failed to kill her with the first blow?* There was no chance I could outrun her.

Frantically, I fumbled through my shepherd's bag and grabbed the first stone I could find.

With the stone in the sling, I sprinted toward the bear. She turned to face me as I charged, releasing the lifeless lamb from her jaws. She rose on her hind legs, towering over me, unleashing a ferocious, snarling roar.

She looked like she was ten feet tall!

"In the name of the Lord!" I shouted, releasing the leather strap. The stone whistled through the air.

I knew I had hit my mark when I heard the dull thud of the stone as it buried itself deep into the bear's skull. I'm not sure who was more surprised—me or the bear. She toppled to the ground like a giant tree felled by a lumberjack. The earth shook beneath my feet as her massive body crashed down. Without hesitation, I drew my knife and slit her throat to ensure she was dead.

"Looks like we'll be eating bear steaks tonight," I murmured.

I bowed my head once more, offering thanks to the Lord for giving me the strength to do the impossible.

Little did I know, yet again, how God was preparing me for a future conflict with a creature that would stand nearly ten feet tall.

Strangely, I never shared the story of the lion and the bear with anyone. I kept it to myself.

THE HARP

W *hat now?* I thought as my brother, Ozem, came running toward me while I sat watching over the sheep on the hillside.

"Please don't tell me Samuel wants to see me again," I said with a slight grin.

"No, it's not Samuel this time," Ozem replied. "It's King Saul!"

My heart skipped a beat, and the grin vanished from my face.

"Does this have anything to do with Samuel anointing me?" I asked, a hint of worry creeping into my voice.

"Why ask me when I don't have the answer?" Ozem snapped, clearly frustrated. "All I know is a messenger came to the house and said King Saul wants to see you. So, grab your things and get going."

"But why? There has to be a reason!" I insisted.

"I don't know what to tell you, except that the messenger said to make sure you bring your harp."

"My harp?"

"Yes. That's all I know. Bring your harp."

When I arrived home, my father had already prepared a donkey, loaded with bread, a skin of wine, and a young goat as gifts for King Saul.

I could see the worry in his eyes, matching my own.

"Dad, why do you think the king wants to see me? Could he know about Samuel anointing me?" I asked, anxiety gripping me.

"I don't know, son," my father replied gravely. "Just keep quiet and do whatever he asks."

During the entire journey, I prayed, seeking comfort in the now familiar calm of the Spirit.

When I arrived at the palace, one of the king's servants met me at the gate, taking the reins of the donkey.

"Did you bring your harp?" the servant asked curtly.

"Yes, I did," I answered. "What is this all about?"

"The king is deeply troubled," the servant replied. "I suggested that music might soothe his mind."

"So, you're the one who sent for me?"

"Yes," the servant confirmed. "When I asked around for a harpist, your name kept coming up. They say you're skillful with the harp, a man of valor, wise with words, and handsome. So, here you are."

"That's quite a reputation to live up to," I said with a nervous chuckle. "I hope I can help. And—did you just call me handsome?" I added with a grin.

The servant wasn't amused.

As I walked through the palace, I was awestruck by its grandeur. *Wow*, I thought, *it must be amazing to live in a place like this.*

I had no idea what the future had in store for me...

When I entered the king's chamber, the curtains were tightly drawn, and Saul lay curled up in bed, the blanket pulled up to his chin. The room was dark—not just because of the drawn curtains, but because a heavy, oppressive spirit filled the air.

Chills ran up my spine.

Saul looked dreadful. His hair was matted and unwashed, and his eyes were sunken with dark circles from nights without sleep.

"Play," he grunted, not bothering to look at me.

I bowed my head and silently prayed for the Lord's anointing. Then, I began to play softly—a song I often played for the sheep when they were restless.

Within moments, I heard the sound of snoring.

I lost count of how many times I was summoned to the palace to play for Saul after that.

THE SLING

"Hey Dad, where are Eliab, Abinadab, and Shammah?" I asked, referring to my three oldest brothers. "I haven't seen them in weeks."

My father's face darkened. "They've been called to fight against the Philistines," he replied.

"Again? It feels like we're always fighting them."

He sighed. "Would you like to go see them and bring them some food?"

"Absolutely!"

"Good. Head back and watch the sheep tonight but come home first thing in the morning. Your mother will have some dried grain and freshly baked bread for your brothers, and cheese for their captain. I want you to deliver the food and then come straight back home."

"Okay," I said. However, I was unaware that this would be my last day as a shepherd.

The next morning, I left the sheep with Ozem and loaded the food my mother had prepared onto a donkey. I was excited at the prospect of seeing my brothers on the battlefield. As I led the donkey, I played my harp, singing a new song the Lord had given me. The Holy Spirit's warmth surrounded me.

But when I approached the camp, all I heard was shouting. The armies of Israel stood on one side of a wide valley, the Philistines on the other. I left the food with the supply keeper and ran towards the commotion. Finding my brothers, I greeted them.

"What's happening?" I asked, puzzled by the chaos.

Before they could respond, a deep, menacing voice echoed across the valley.

"Who's that?" I asked, squinting to see the source of the voice.

19

"That's Goliath," Eliab said, visibly shaken. "The Philistine champion."

"So?" I replied.

Eliab shot me a look. "Have you seen him? He's a giant."

"So?" I repeated.

"He's over nine feet tall!"

"So?"

"The sword he carries probably weighs more than you do!"

"And?"

Frustrated, Eliab continued, "And... he's challenged us to send someone to fight him, one-on-one."

I was confused. How could the great armies of Israel be paralyzed by fear over one man?

"How long has this been going on?" I asked.

"Forty days," Eliab said grimly.

"Forty days? And no one's accepted his challenge?"

Eliab scoffed. "Are you volunteering?"

Ignoring his sarcasm, I asked, "What does the man who defeats him get?"

A nearby soldier, missing several teeth, grinned. "The king's offering great riches, his daughter's hand in marriage, and exemption from taxes for his family."

I paused for a moment. "Who is this uncircumcised Philistine that he should defy the armies of the living God?"

Eliab, now irritated, stepped closer. "Why are you even here? And who's watching the sheep?"

I didn't flinch. "I came to bring you food, and the sheep are taken care of. The real question is, why isn't anyone doing anything about that giant?"

Eliab glared at me. "I know why you're here. It's your pride and arrogance. You just want to watch the battle."

I wasn't fazed. "No, I'm not. Is there not a cause?"

"What?" Eliab asked, bewildered.

"Is there not a reason to fight this giant?"

Several soldiers grinned at me, as if I were a naive child. However, I wouldn't back down.

"What about the rest of you?" I shouted at the soldiers. "Is there not a cause?"

One of them called out, "Are you willing to fight him?"

"You bet I am!" I replied.

"Seriously?"

"Yes!"

The soldier ran to tell King Saul what I'd said. Meanwhile, my brothers stood glaring at me. I didn't care. I couldn't believe that the army of Israel was cowering before one Philistine—even if he was a giant.

Moments later, the soldier returned. "The king wants to see you."

Still fired up, I was brought before Saul.

"Why is everyone so afraid of this giant?" I asked him. "I'm not afraid. Let me fight him!"

Saul, amused, chuckled. "Who do you think you are, kid? You're just a boy, and he's been a warrior since his youth."

I took a deep breath. "Your majesty, may I tell you a story?"

Saul nodded, still entertained.

"I'm a shepherd," I began. "One day, a lion took one of my father's lambs. After the Spirit of the Lord came upon me, I pursued the lion, grabbed it by the beard, and killed it. Another time, a bear attacked the flock. The Lord empowered me again, and I killed the bear. I've killed both lion and bear, and this Philistine will be no different. He's defied the armies of the living God. The same God who delivered me from the lion and the bear will deliver me from him!"

Saul's amusement faded. "You're serious?"

"Yes," I replied.

After a pause, Saul said, "May the Lord be with you. If you're determined, I won't stop you."

Saul led me to his chariot and handed me his armor. I tried it on, but it was far too big. The soldiers laughed as I struggled with the heavy gear.

"Thanks, but no thanks," I said, removing the armor. "I haven't tested these."

Saul asked, "What will you take?"

I held up my sling and patted my shepherd's bag. "These… and the Lord."

With that, I set off toward Goliath. As I crossed a brook, I selected five smooth stones, placing them in my bag.

The Holy Spirit's presence was with me.

When Goliath saw me, he sneered. "Am I a dog, that you come at me with sticks?"

He cursed me by his gods. "Come here, boy! I'll feed your flesh to the birds and beasts!"

But I wasn't afraid. I shouted back, "You come against me with sword, spear, and javelin, but I come against you in the name of the Lord of hosts, the God of the armies of Israel, whom you have defied. Today, the Lord will deliver you into my hands!"

Goliath roared with laughter. "Come on, then!"

Reaching into my bag, I took out a stone, placed it in my sling, and ran toward him. The armies of Israel and Philistia were both transfixed.

"Go David! Go David!" I heard the Israelites chanting.

I swung my sling and with all my might and with a prayer I released the stone. It struck Goliath's forehead with a thud. His eyes widened in shock as he fell forward, crashing into the dirt.

A roar erupted from the Israelite soldiers!

I ran to Goliath, drew his own sword, and with a single blow, severed his head. The Philistines, seeing their champion dead, fled in terror as the Israelite army pursued them.

Gallantly, I took Goliath's head to Saul and threw it at his feet. He stared at me in amazement.

"Who are you? Have we met before?" he asked.

"I am David, son of your servant Jesse of Bethlehem," I replied.

Saul's eyes narrowed, and a chill ran up my spine. I knew then—I had caught the king's attention. And for some reason, I wasn't sure that was a good thing.

DAVID MEETS JONATHAN

After I killed Goliath, my whole world changed. Saul insisted that I remain in Jerusalem, residing in the king's palace. Gone were the days of watching sheep; instead, I found myself captivated by the abundance of servants and the lavish feasts served daily.

It was there that God blessed me with a surprising friendship. Of all people, a friendship blossomed with Jonathan, the son of King Saul. Initially, Jonathan was likely pleased because I had killed Goliath and was willing to play my harp to soothe his father when he was distressed. But as time passed and I took up residence in the palace, our bond grew much deeper.

One day, Jonathan pulled me aside, his expression earnest. "Here," he said, handing me his robe. "This is a special robe my father gave me, but I want you to have it. And I know my father's armor didn't fit you, so take mine. We're about the same size."

I hesitated. "Oh no, Jonathan, I can't. What will you do for armor?"

He laughed warmly. "Don't worry. The blacksmith still has my measurements. I've already arranged for another set. And I want you to have my bow, arrows, and this hand-crafted leather belt as well."

"Jonathan," I protested, "this is too much. These things are your personal treasures."

He smiled. "That's exactly why I want you to have them. They're a special gift to show how much your friendship means to me."

I was deeply moved by his generosity. Looking back, I now realize that Jonathan must have understood that God's anointing was shifting from Saul to me. Yet, throughout our friendship, he never displayed a hint of jealousy or resentment.

As time passed, it became increasingly clear to me that God had indeed withdrawn His favor from Saul. The king seemed perpetually angry or depressed. I quickly learned that it was best to comply with any request Saul made of me, no matter how trivial.

In the beginning, Saul was grateful that I had killed the giant and played my harp to calm him. He even promoted me to a high position in his army, which earned me favor with the people, as well as with Saul's servants. As a commander, the Lord's anointing was with me in every battle, and I found favor with my fellow soldiers. Everything seemed to be going well.

However, that all changed after one particular victory over the Philistines. It had been a triumphant day, and I had slain an astounding number of the enemy. The women of the city came out to greet us, dancing and singing with tambourines and other instruments. They sang, *"Saul has slain his thousands, and David his tens of thousands."*

Saul, mounted on his white stallion, turned to me with a look that sent a chill down my spine—anger and jealousy radiated from him. He muttered to his armor-bearer, loud enough for me to hear, *"They credit David with killing tens of thousands and me with only thousands. What's next? Will they make him king?"*

I knew then that things had taken a dark turn.

The very next day, I received an order from Saul. He appointed me over a battalion of one thousand soldiers. At first, I thought it was a reward for my loyalty, but I soon realized Saul was hoping I'd be killed in battle. However, the Lord was with me in every fight. The greater the challenge, the greater the victory. And as I excelled in battle, Saul's resentment toward me grew stronger. To make matters worse, the soldiers increasingly praised me with each campaign I led.

DAVID GETS MARRIED

O ne day, after returning from yet another victorious battle, King Saul summoned me. I hurried to see what he wanted.

"David," Saul began, "here is my eldest daughter, Merab. I have decided to give her to you in marriage. In return, I want your promise that you will serve me bravely and fight the battles of the Lord."

I was taken aback.

"Thank you," I replied. "I promise!"

But I sensed deception. I suspected that Saul's offer was just a ploy to keep me engaged in battle for as long as possible. I could almost hear his thoughts: *Why raise my own hand against David when the Philistines can do it for me?*

Despite Saul's ill intentions, I maintained my humility before him.

"Who am I," I responded to his offer, "and what is my family or my clan in Israel, that I should become the king's son-in-law?"

"Don't worry about that," Saul said dismissively. "I simply want you to marry my daughter."

Yet my instincts proved correct. When the time came for Merab to marry me, Saul reneged on his promise, and she was given to Adriel of Meholah instead. Surprisingly, I felt a sense of relief. Merab seemed kind, but neither of us harbored love for one another.

It was a different story, however, with Saul's younger daughter, Michal. Every time we were together, I could sense her growing fondness for me, and before long, I found myself developing feelings for her as well.

I was astonished when Saul noticed our attraction and offered Michal's hand in marriage.

"You now have a second opportunity to become my son-in-law," Saul said with a smirk.

While I was pleased by his offer, I wasn't naive. I knew Saul was still scheming, even if it meant using his daughter to entrap me.

To sway me further, Saul even sent his attendants to flatter me, which I found amusing.

"Look," one of them said, "I know the king has acted against you in the past, but deep down, he genuinely likes you. And not only that—all of us, his attendants, love you too. Why hesitate in becoming his son-in-law?"

"Listen," I told the attendant, "Marriage is a significant decision, and marrying the king's daughter even more so. I am but a simple shepherd from a poor family. I wonder if I truly belong in the royal family?"

The servant relayed my words back to Saul, who then sent him to me again with a message.

"David," he said, "King Saul is so eager for you to marry Michal that he has waived the dowry. All he asks is that you kill one hundred Philistines and bring him their foreskins."

I couldn't help but raise an eyebrow. "Really? All he wants for a dowry are the foreskins of a hundred Philistines? I get to slay some enemies *and* marry Michal?"

The servant chuckled. "Strange as it sounds, that's exactly what he said."

I immediately recognized Saul's deceit. He hoped I would be killed in the process. If I died at the hands of the Philistines, Saul could wash his hands of any blame. Yet, despite this, the prospect of marrying Michal pleased me. So, I accepted Saul's offer.

Understanding that Saul intended for me to die in this venture, I took a group of my men along for support. Instead of bringing back one hundred Philistine foreskins, I returned with two hundred!

When King Saul saw what I had accomplished and that I had survived, he realized he had no choice but to honor his promise. Michal and I were married.

Once again, Saul's plot to kill me had failed.

With every unsuccessful attempt on my life, Saul became more aware that the Spirit of the Lord was indeed with me. But instead of finding peace in that knowledge, his anger only deepened.

SAUL OPENLY THREATENS DAVID

"Hey, Brother-In-Law!" Jonathan shouted as he wrapped me in a giant hug. "Congratulations! I'm so happy you're officially part of the family!"

"Thanks!" I replied, though a little uncertain. "But honestly, I'm not sure your father feels the same way."

Jonathan's joyful expression faltered, his face clouding with concern. "Yeah, about that… I came to warn you. My father told me, and his servants, to watch you closely—and if we get the chance, to take your life."

The truth was out: Saul wanted me dead, and he wasn't hiding it anymore.

"He said that?" I asked, my brows knitting together in disbelief.

Jonathan nodded grimly. "Yes, I've never seen him like this with anyone. Be careful. My advice is to hide until he cools off."

"What have I done, Jonathan?" I asked, frustration evident in my voice. "Why does your father hate me so much?"

Jonathan shook his head. "It's not you—it's his jealousy. You're loved by the people and admired for your victories. That's enough to make him feel threatened."

He continued, "I'll talk to him. I hate to say it, but it's probably best that you go into hiding while I try to reason with him. I'll let you know what he says."

I was grateful, but also worried for Jonathan's safety. "Thank you," I said, my voice breaking. "I don't know what I'd do without you."

Jonathan's eyes glistened with tears. "You know I'll do anything to resolve this. You're my best friend."

The next day, I waited anxiously. *What would happen if Saul still wanted to kill me? Would I have to leave Michal and go into hiding?* My mind raced with possibilities until I saw Jonathan running toward me, smiling.

"Father gave me his word," Jonathan said, breathless. "As surely as the Lord lives, he no longer wants you dead."

Relief washed over me. "How did you convince him?"

"I reminded him of your loyalty—how you risked your life against Goliath for his sake and for Israel's victory. I asked him point-blank why he'd want to kill an innocent man. And he swore to leave you alone."

"And he gave you his oath?" I pressed.

Jonathan nodded. "Yes. You can come home."

That day, peace returned, and I made my way back to the palace, rejoicing and singing to the Lord.

But the peace was short-lived. War broke out again with the Philistines, and once more, the Spirit of the Lord was with me. We secured another victory, and Saul's jealousy flared up again.

I hoped for the best and brought my harp to play for him, praying that music might soothe his spirit like it once had. But as soon as I saw Saul, sitting with his spear in hand and a dark look in his eyes, I knew it was a mistake.

As I played, I kept one eye on him, just in case. It saved my life—Saul suddenly leaped up and hurled his spear at me! I dodged it, and the spear lodged in the wall. I fled once more.

"Where is he?!" Saul bellowed as he stormed through the palace. "I'll kill him with my own hands!"

He ordered his men to watch my house. When they arrived, Michal, my wife, warned me, "If you don't escape tonight, you'll be killed by morning."

She let me down through a window, and I fled. Michal then laid an idol in our bed, disguising it with a garment and goat's hair to make it look like I was there.

The next morning, Saul's soldiers knocked on the door. "Where is David?" they demanded.

"He's sick," Michal replied.

When they reported this to Saul, he snapped, "Bring him to me in his bed so I can kill him myself!"

The soldiers returned, only to find the idol in my place.

Furious, Saul confronted Michal. "Why did you betray me like this?" he spat.

Michal stood her ground. "Father, David is not your enemy. Why are you trying to kill him? He's the man I love!"

But Saul, consumed by hatred, ignored her.

Soon after, Saul sent men to capture me in Ramah, but something unexpected happened. As they approached, they saw a group of prophets with Samuel, and the Spirit of God came upon them—they began to prophesy instead of arresting me!

When Saul heard this, he sent more men, but the same thing happened. Furious, Saul sent a third group, but they too were overcome by the Spirit of God. Finally, Saul went himself. To everyone's amazement, he too began prophesying and ended up lying naked before the Lord all day and night!

His soldiers whispered among themselves, *"Is this a sign from God to stop pursuing David?"*

Despite God's obvious attempt to soothe Saul, I wisely chose not to confront him. Instead, I returned to Jonathan. Falling to my knees, I wept before him. "What have I done?" I cried. "Why is your father so determined to kill me?"

Jonathan knelt beside me, pulling me into an embrace. "You won't die, David. I swear I'll protect you. My father wouldn't hide anything from me. I'll find out what's happening."

But I knew better. "Jonathan, he knows you care for me. He's keeping his plans from you. As surely as the Lord lives, there's only a step between me and death."

Jonathan's voice softened. "Tell me what you want me to do, and I'll do it."

"Tomorrow is the New Moon feast," I said. "I'm supposed to be there, but I'll hide in the field instead. If your father notices my absence, tell him I went to Bethlehem for a family sacrifice. If he's fine with it, we'll know I'm safe. But if he's angry, we'll know he still wants me dead."

Jonathan agreed, and I clasped his shoulders. "Your friendship means everything to me," I said. "If I'm guilty of any crime, then kill me yourself. I'd rather die by your hand than by your father's."

Overcome with emotion and torn between his love for me and his love and devotion to his father, Jonathan sobbed, "David, I am speaking from my heart. Honestly, if I had even the slightest inkling that my father was seriously determined to harm you, wouldn't I tell you?"

Seeing the difficult position Jonathan was in, I responded, "Listen, let's go ahead with our plan and then you tell me if your father answers you harshly?"

Wiping the tears from his face, Jonathan said, "Okay. Can we just go for a walk out in the field."

"Sure," I responded, wiping the tears from my face as well.

"This brings back a lot of memories," I stated, as we made our way to a hilltop covered with deep luscious green grass, blowing in the wind. It was a beautiful day. The sun was shining, and birds were chirping in the nearby trees. The contrast of the calmness of nature around us and the unrest in my soul was contradictory.

Jonathan smiled at me. "Does this bring back memories of when you were a shepherd boy?"

"Yes." I responded. "Life was so much simpler then."

"I am so sorry for the way things have turned out between you and my father," Jonathan said, "And I swear by the Lord, the God of Israel, that I will surely sound out my father by this time the day after tomorrow! If he is favorably disposed toward you, I give you my promise that I will send word to you and let you know. But if I sense my father intends to harm you, may the Lord deal with me ever so severely, if I do not let you know and send you away in peace."

We sat there for several minutes in silence. We both sensed that this was a moment in our relationship that we would cherish for years to come.

Breaking the silence Jonathan said softly, "David, will you make me a promise?"

"Sure," I replied.

"Will you promise to show me and my family unfailing kindness like the Lord's kindness as long as I live, so that I may not be killed, and will you promise to never cut off your kindness from my family—not even when the Lord has cut off every one of your enemies from the face of the earth?"

"Oh my," I responded, deeply moved in my spirit. "Yes! Absolutely yes!"

So, on that day Jonathan and I made a covenant together, saying, *"May the Lord call David's enemies to account."*

Then, just to make sure there was no misunderstanding, Jonathan had me reaffirm my oath.

I did so enthusiastically.

Once more Jonathan shared his great love for me and our deep friendship, stating that he loved me as he loved himself.

We sat there in silence, not wanting the moment to end.

Finally, Jonathan broke the silence and said, "Well, tomorrow is the New Moon feast. Just know that you will be greatly missed, because your seat will be empty."

"Yes, I will most certainly miss being there as well," I replied.

Jonathan continued, "So, the day after tomorrow, toward evening, go to the place where you hid when this trouble began, and wait by the stone Ezel. Here is what I will do, I will shoot three arrows to the side of it, as though I were shooting at a target. Then I will send a boy to find them. If I say to him, 'Look, the arrows are on this side of you; bring them here,' then you will know it's okay to come out of hiding, because, as surely as the Lord lives, you are safe and there is no danger. But if I say to the boy, 'Look, the arrows are beyond you', then you must go, because the Lord has sent you away."

Once more tears swelled in my eyes. "Okay, dear friend, it sounds like a plan."

"And about the matter you and I discussed concerning me and my family," Jonathan continued, "remember, the Lord is witness between you and me forever."

"I will never forget," I responded, embracing Jonathan.

When Jonathan returned home, he heard the servants talking about what happened when Saul sent men to find me at Ramah, and how all three groups of men began prophesying instead.

"Even your father prophesied when he went there," one of the servants told Jonathan.

"Seriously?" Jonathan responded, not quite sure what to think.

Maybe… just maybe… Jonathan thought, *maybe this spiritual experience has changed my father's heart.*

That evening King Saul took his customary place at the table, with his back to the wall. Jonathan took his customary place directly across the table from his father. However, my seat sat empty.

Jonathan waited for his father to talk about his experience at Ramah or make a comment about my empty chair. However, Saul said nothing that day, he just sat there eating with his head down as if deep in thought.

When Saul said nothing about my absence, Jonathan reasoned to himself that Saul thought maybe something had happened to me to make me ceremonially unclean and that was why I wasn't there.

The next day, the second day of the month, my chair at the table was empty again. This time Saul looked sternly across the table at Jonathan and asked, "Why hasn't the son of Jesse come to the meal, either yesterday or today?"

Jonathan cleared his throat and answered, "David earnestly asked me for permission to go to Bethlehem. He said, 'Let me go, because our family is observing a sacrifice in the town and my brother has ordered me to be there. If I have found favor in your eyes, let me get away to see my brothers.' That is why he has not come to the king's table."

Saul's demeanor slowly changed. His face started turning red as the blood flooded into his face.

Suddenly he leaped to his feet, kicking his chair away. Glaring down at Jonathan he growled at him, "You son of a perverse and rebellious woman! I know that you have sided with the son of Jesse to your own shame and to the shame of the mother who bore you! How dare you?"

Jonathan sat there in horror, cowering before the madman his father had become right before his very eyes.

"As long as that son of Jesse lives on this earth," Saul snarled, "Neither you nor your kingdom will be established. Don't you understand that? When I am gone the kingdom should be rightfully yours! Don't you get that? Now, send someone to bring him to me, for he must die!"

Jonathan gathered all the strength he could, and facing his father he shouted "Why should David be put to death? Seriously, what has he done?"

Then Saul completely lost all sense of reality and Jonathan witnessed firsthand the evil that his father had allowed to enter his heart. Turning, Saul ran to where his spear was leaning against the wall. He grabbed it and turned back to where Jonathan was sitting. Jonathan could not believe what was happening. Surely his father would not attempt to kill him! However, Saul did exactly that. He hurled his spear at his very own son with all his might! Jonathan ducked as the spear flew past him, barely missing its target.

Then Jonathan knew without a doubt that his father intended to kill me. Jonathan got up from the table in fierce anger and walked away, grieving at his father's shameful treatment of himself and me.

That night Jonathan tossed and turned in his bed. Sleep evaded him as he sought for an answer from the Lord. *Who is this mad man that was once so humble and kind*, he thought. *What has happened to the loving father I knew as a child?*

The next morning Jonathan rose early and went out to the field for his meeting with me. He had a small boy with him.

Just as planned Jonathan said to the boy, "Run and find the arrows I shoot."

As the boy ran, Jonathan shot an arrow beyond him. When the boy came to the place where Jonathan's arrow had fallen Jonathan called out after him, "Isn't the arrow beyond you? Hurry! Go quickly! Don't stop!" The boy found the arrow and returned to Jonathan. Jonathan gave his bow and arrows to the boy and said, "Go, take my bow and arrows back home."

I knew what this meant. I knew that things had not gone well with Saul.

After the boy was gone, I got up from the south side of the stone and looked across the meadow at my dear friend. I bowed down before him three times with my face to the ground.

35

It was more than Jonathan could stand. Forgetting that one of his father's servants may have followed him, he ran to me with all his might, embracing me in the deep bonds of friendship. We kissed each other on the cheek and wept together. But I think I wept the most.

With a trembling voice Jonathan said to me, "Go in peace, for we have sworn friendship with each other in the name of the Lord, saying, 'The Lord is witness between you and me, and between your descendants and my descendants forever.'"

Reluctantly, I turned and slowly walked away, and Jonathan turned and slowly walked back home.

Stopping beneath a juniper tree, I fell on my face before God and cried out to him.

Pulling a piece of parchment and a pen from my shepherd's bag I began to write:

Judge me, O Lord; for I have walked in mine integrity:
I have trusted also in the Lord; therefore I shall not slide.
Examine me, O Lord, and prove me; try my reins and my heart.
For Thy lovingkindness is before mine eyes: and I have walked in
Thy truth.

I have not sat with vain persons, neither will I go in with
dissemblers.
I have hated the congregation of evil doers; and will not sit with the
wicked.
I will wash mine hands in innocency: so will I compass Thine altar, O
Lord: That I may publish with the voice of thanksgiving, and tell of
all Thy wondrous works.

Lord, I have loved the habitation of Thy house, and the place where
Thine honour dwelleth.
Gather not my soul with sinners, nor my life with bloody men: In
whose hands is mischief, and their right hand is full of bribes.

But as for me, I will walk in mine integrity: redeem me, and be
merciful unto me.

My foot standeth in an even place: in the congregations will I bless the Lord.
(Psalm 26 KJV)

DAVID GOES ON THE RUN

I wasn't sure what to do next. I knew I could never return to King Saul's house, nor could I go back to the home Michal and I shared. Returning to my father's house was also out of the question; Saul's men would surely find me there.

Once again, I was overwhelmed by the same feelings I had battled as a young boy—feelings of isolation, inadequacy, and neglect. These emotions crashed over me like a giant wave.

In my despair, I did the only thing I knew to do: I fell on my face before the Lord and prayed:

> *In the Lord put I my trust: how say ye to my soul, Flee as a bird to your mountain?*
> *For, lo, the wicked bend their bow, they make ready their arrow upon the string, that they may privily shoot at the upright in heart.*
> *If the foundations be destroyed, what can the righteous do?*
>
> *The Lord is in His holy temple, the Lord's throne is in heaven: His eyes behold, His eyelids try, the children of men.*
> *The Lord trieth the righteous: but the wicked and him that loveth violence His soul hateth.*
> *Upon the wicked He shall rain snares, fire and brimstone, and an horrible tempest: this shall be the portion of their cup.*
>
> *For the righteous Lord loveth righteousness; His countenance doth behold the upright.*
> *(Psalm 11 KJV)*

After praying, I decided to go to Nob to see Ahimelek the priest.

When Ahimelek saw me approaching, he began to tremble. "Is that really you, David?" he asked.

"Yes, it's me," I replied with a smile.

"Why are you alone? Why is no one with you?" the priest asked, catching me off guard.

Ashamed, I stumbled over my words and lied. "Well…King Saul sent me on a secret mission and told me, 'No one is to know anything about this mission I am sending you on.' As for my men, I've instructed them to meet me later at a certain place."

To change the subject, I quickly added, "Do you have anything here to eat? I'll take whatever you have on hand. Just give me a few loaves of bread, or whatever you can find for me and my men."

The priest looked around and answered, "I'm sorry, I don't have any ordinary bread, but there is some consecrated bread—provided you and your men have kept yourselves from women."

I assured him, "Oh, you don't have to worry about that. We've kept ourselves away from women as we always do when we're on a mission."

Nodding in approval, the priest gave me the consecrated bread.

Standing in the corner was Doeg the Edomite, Saul's chief shepherd, listening to every word of our conversation. I felt uneasy with him being there, but if Ahimelek didn't mind, I figured it was no concern of mine.

As Ahimelek gathered the bread, I lied a second time. "Do you have a spear or sword here? I didn't bring any weapons because the king's mission was urgent."

Grinning, the priest enthusiastically replied, "I do! The sword of Goliath the Philistine, whom you killed in the Valley of Elah, is here!"

"You've got to be kidding me!" I exclaimed, breaking into a grin. "You have Goliath's sword?"

"Yes," Ahimelek grinned, "there's no other sword like it. It's wrapped in a cloth behind the ephod. If you want it, take it. There's no other sword here."

Beaming, I said, "You're right, there's none like it; give it to me."

Sure enough, it was Goliath's sword—the same sword I last held when I took Goliath's life.

Gathering the bread and the sword, I left and made my way to where my men were waiting. As we ate the bread, the men took turns holding and admiring Goliath's sword. Some of them, like little children, swung the giant sword around, pretending to defeat an enemy.

As they laughed and joked, I began discussing our next move with them. After several suggestions, one of the men proposed, "Hey, we have Goliath's sword. Why not go to Goliath's hometown?"

"Gath?" I questioned. "You're suggesting we hide out in Gath?"

"Well, think about it," he replied. "That's the last place Saul would think of looking for us!"

"That may be true," I conceded, "but... GATH???"

After a heated discussion, I finally agreed that we would hide out in Goliath's hometown for a while.

***

"Hey, King!" a servant shouted to Achish, the king of Gath. "You'll never believe who's been spotted entering our territory."

"Who?"

"We're pretty sure it's David."

"Which David?"

"Come on, King, how many David's do you know? It's the same David rumored to be the next king of Israel. The same David the women of Israel love to sing and dance for. The same David who killed our famous warrior Goliath!"

"I'll have to see that to believe it! Why would he be venturing into our territory?"

King Achish took several soldiers with him to check us out.

When I saw King Achish walking toward us, squinting as if trying to recognize me, I realized that we might have been found out. He acted as if he knew who I was!

What should I do? I thought frantically. I knew what would happen if we were discovered.

What to do… what to do? I kept thinking.

I know—I'll pretend to be mad!

As King Achish approached, I quickly curled up next to the doorway of a small hut, scratching at the door with my fingernails and drooling down my beard. I scratched so violently that marks were left in the doorway, and splinters of wood lodged under my fingernails.

Backing away, King Achish turned and snarled to his servants, "This isn't David! This man is insane! Am I so short of madmen that you bring this fellow to carry on like this in front of me? Do you really think I'll allow this man into my house or let him stay in our land? Madness is contagious! Get him out of my sight!"

It worked!

"Get this madman out of here!" one of King Achish's soldiers shouted to my men. "You heard the king. And don't come back!"

Seeing that we were free to go, my men and I quickly left the city.

Once we were outside the city limits, we started laughing.

"That was ingenious!" one of my men said.

"Yeah," another chimed in. "David, you really did look crazy. How many splinters are under your fingernails? You were scratching that doorway like a dog with fleas!"

"And" another added, "I loved the way you drooled all over yourself! You really did look mad!"

The men were now laughing hysterically.

"The craziest part of all this," I admitted, "is that we had Goliath's sword with us! What were we thinking???"

At that, my men doubled over in laughter, pounding each other on the back.

After they finally settled down, I said, "Well… that didn't work. Anyone else have any bright ideas? Where should we go now?"

As we walked along the road, discussing several places to hide, I suddenly stopped.

"I've got it!" I shouted. "I don't know why I didn't think of this before. When I was a kid taking care of my dad's sheep, I stumbled upon a cave called the Cave of Adullam."

"And you don't think Saul or his men will find us there?" one of the men asked.

"No. Think about it… we'll be hiding right under their noses!"

"And it's within walking distance of my father's house," I added, "so my family can visit me!"

"Are you sure it's big enough for all of us?" another man asked. "You're growing quite famous and have a large following."

"Oh yes," I exclaimed. "It's a huge cave!"

***

As soon as we arrived at the cave, word spread that I was there with my trusted soldiers. Those in distress, in debt, or discontented began gathering with us, and I became their commander. Within a few days, at least four hundred men had joined our forces.

However, I knew that with a group this large, sooner or later, Saul would hear of our location. After consulting with my men, I decided we should go to Mizpah in Moab.

As we prepared to leave, a young man came running up.

"Where's David?" he demanded angrily.

I stepped forward and asked, "Here I am. Who are you?"

"I am Abiathar, the son of Ahimelek, the priest at Nob," the young man replied.

"How is your father?" I asked, remembering how he had helped us.

"He's DEAD!" the young man blurted out.

"Dead? What happened?" I asked, shocked.

Tearfully, Abiathar recounted how King Saul and his men had shown up and questioned his father about me and my men.

"My father told King Saul what you told him—that you were on a secret mission from the king. But Saul exploded in rage, calling my father a liar. Is it true? Did you lie to my father?"

I slowly dropped my head in shame. "Yes, it's true."

Abiathar's face contorted with anger. "Because of what you told my father, King Saul ordered his men to kill every priest at Nob! When they refused, Saul ordered Doeg the Edomite, who was there the day you came, to do it. He murdered all eighty-five of the priests, including my father. Afterward, he slaughtered all the men, women, children, and even the livestock of the entire town. I barely escaped with my life."

Crying out in anguish, I told Abiathar, "I knew that when Doeg the Edomite was there, he would be sure to tell Saul. Listen, I confess. I am the one responsible for the death of your whole family. However, I plead with you, stay with me; don't be afraid. The man who wants to kill you is trying to kill me too. You will be safe with me."

At first, he hesitated, but then replied, "Okay," collapsing into my arms.

After consoling him, I turned to my men and said, "Listen, if Abiathar could find us, so can Saul. We need to move quickly."

"What are you thinking?" one of the men asked.

"I think we should head to Mizpah in Moab."

"That's a long journey," the man replied. "It's across the Dead Sea, between Edom and Ammon. It'll take at least seven or eight days. But it sounds like a good plan."

"I agree," I said. "But I'm concerned Saul might harm my parents. I'd like to take them with us. I can easily see Saul taking his hatred for me out on them."

Everyone agreed.

"Now, if you don't mind," I continued, "I need to be alone."

Respectfully, the men retreated from the cave, leaving me to speak with the Lord. In my despair, I sat down and began to write:

> *I cried unto the Lord with my voice; with my voice unto the Lord did I make my supplication.*

I poured out my complaint before Him; I shewed before Him my trouble.

When my spirit was overwhelmed within me, then Thou knewest my path.
In the way wherein I walked have they privily laid a snare for me.
I looked on my right hand, and beheld but there was no man that would know me: refuge failed me; no man cared for my soul.

I cried unto Thee, O Lord: I said, Thou art my refuge and my portion in the land of the living.
Attend unto my cry; for I am brought very low: deliver me from my persecutors; for they are stronger than I.
Bring my soul out of prison, that I may praise Thy name:
The righteous shall compass me about; for Thou shalt deal bountifully with me.
(Psalm 142 KJV)

Once more, I found comfort and peace in the presence of the Lord.

As we journeyed to Moab, I began to reminisce about the story my mother told me about my great-grandmother Ruth, and how she came from the land of Moab. As we walked, I began singing another new song:

"Hear my voice, O God, in my prayer: preserve my life from fear of the enemy.
Hide me from the secret counsel of the wicked; from the insurrection of the workers of iniquity: who whet their tongue like a sword, and bend their bows to shoot their arrows, even bitter words:
That they may shoot in secret at the perfect: suddenly do they shoot at him, and fear not.

"They encourage themselves in an evil matter: they commune of laying snares privily; They say, Who shall see them?
They search out iniquities; they accomplish a diligent search:
Both the inward thought of every one of them, and the heart, is deep.

*But God shall shoot at them with an arrow; suddenly shall they be
wounded.*
*So they shall make their own tongue to fall upon themselves: all
that see them shall flee away.*
*And all men shall fear, and shall declare the work of God; For they
shall wisely consider of His doing.*

*"The righteous shall be glad in the Lord, and shall trust in Him; And
all the upright in heart shall glory."*
(Psalm 64 KJV)

By the time we arrived in Moab, the whole army was singing, *"The
righteous will rejoice in the Lord and take refuge in Him,"* right along with
me.

Upon our arrival, I went to see the king of Moab. He knew the story of my
great-grandmother Ruth.

"O King," I asked, bowing respectfully, "will you please allow my father and
mother to stay here in the land of Moab until I hear from God what to do
next?"

"Of course," the king replied, "they may stay as long as they wish! We are
honored to have you here. Everyone knows the great love story of Ruth
and Boaz."

It was comforting to walk the same streets my great-grandmother had
walked when she was young. As I sought God's guidance on what to do
next, a prophet of Gad approached me.

"David, we're glad you're here," the prophet said, "but I don't think you
should stay in the stronghold of Moab. The Lord wants you to go into the
land of Judah."

"Let me think and pray about it," I responded. After spending time in
prayer, I decided the prophet was right. So, we left and went to the forest
of Hereth in Judah.

When we arrived in Hereth, I received word that the Philistines were
fighting against Keilah and looting their threshing floors. Once more, I
sought the Lord in prayer.

"Shall I go and attack these Philistines?" I inquired of the Lord.

The Lord answered, *"Yes, go, attack the Philistines and save Keilah."*

However, when I told my men what the Lord had said, they were afraid.

"Are you sure about this?" one of them challenged.

So, I inquired of the Lord again, and He answered a second time, *"Go down to Keilah, for I am going to give the Philistines into your hand!"*

I approached my men once more. "I know you're reluctant to fight against the Philistines, and I understand, but the Lord has reassured me that He will go with us and grant us a great victory. Do you trust me?"

Seeing the confidence in my eyes, the men agreed to go and fight the Philistines. And the Lord was indeed with us. We inflicted heavy losses on the Philistines and saved the people of Keilah.

As we marched away in victory, I broke out into another song:

"In Thee, O Lord, do I put my trust; let me never be ashamed: deliver me in Thy righteousness.
Bow down Thine ear to me; deliver me speedily: be Thou my strong rock, for an house of defence to save me.

"For Thou art my rock and my fortress; therefore for Thy name's sake lead me, and guide me.
Pull me out of the net that they have laid privily for me: for Thou art my strength.
Into Thine hand I commit my spirit: Thou hast redeemed me, O Lord God of truth.

"I have hated them that regard lying vanities: but I trust in the Lord.
I will be glad and rejoice in Thy mercy: for Thou hast considered my trouble; Thou hast known my soul in adversities; and hast not shut me up into the hand of the enemy:
Thou hast set my feet in a large room.

"Have mercy upon me, O Lord, for I am in trouble:
Mine eye is consumed with grief, yea, my soul and my belly.
For my life is spent with grief, and my years with sighing:

My strength faileth because of mine iniquity, and my bones are
consumed.
I was a reproach among all mine enemies, but especially among my
neighbours, and a fear to mine acquaintance: they that did see me
without fled from me.
I am forgotten as a dead man out of mind: I am like a broken
vessel.
For I have heard the slander of many: fear was on every side:
While they took counsel together against me, they devised to take
away my life.

"But I trusted in Thee, O Lord: I said, Thou art my God.
My times are in Thy hand: deliver me from the hand of mine
enemies, and from them that persecute me.
Make Thy face to shine upon Thy servant: save me for Thy mercies'
sake.
Let me not be ashamed, O Lord; for I have called upon Thee: let the
wicked be ashamed, and let them be silent in the grave.
Let the lying lips be put to silence; which speak grievous things
proudly and contemptuously against the righteous.

"Oh how great is Thy goodness, which Thou hast laid up for them
that fear thee; which Thou hast wrought for them that trust in Thee
before the sons of men!
Thou shalt hide them in the secret of Thy presence from the pride of
man: Thou shalt keep them secretly in a pavilion from the strife of
tongues.

"Blessed be the Lord: for He hath shewed me His marvelous
kindness in a strong city.
For I said in my haste, I am cut off from before Thine eyes:
nevertheless Thou heardest the voice of my supplications
when I cried unto Thee.

"O love the Lord, all ye His saints: for the Lord preserveth the
faithful, and plentifully rewardeth the proud doer.
Be of good courage, and He shall strengthen your heart,
All ye that hope in the Lord."
(Psalm 31 KJV)

JONATHAN VISITS DAVID

"God has delivered David into my hands," Saul sneered to those near him, an evil grin spreading across his face. "David has sealed his fate now... I know exactly where he is. He's trapped himself by entering the town of Keilah, with its gates and bars."

Saul then mustered all his forces to march down to Keilah, intent on attacking me and my men. "I've got him now," Saul snarled. "There's no way he'll escape this time!"

However, once again, the Lord revealed Saul's plot to me. I immediately went to Abiathar the priest and said, "Please bring me the ephod of the Lord." (An ephod is like an apron.)

Reverently, I placed the ephod around my waist.

Once more, the Spirit of the Lord came upon me, and I knelt in prayer, *"Lord, God of Israel, I know Saul is planning to come to Keilah and destroy the town because of me. Lord, I have a question for You. Will the citizens of Keilah betray me and surrender me to him? Lord, God of Israel, tell Your servant."*

The Lord replied, *"Yes, they will."*

Rising to my feet, I shouted, "Let's go, men!" to the six hundred men who were with me. We immediately left Keilah, and from that moment on, we moved constantly from one place to another.

When Saul learned that I had left Keilah, he flew into another fit of rage, yelling and screaming at everyone around him. He likely suspected there was a spy in his camp. However, the "spy" was the Lord!

Meanwhile, my men and I moved from stronghold to stronghold in the hills of the Desert of Ziph, always on the move. Day after day, Saul continued searching for us, but God watched over us and did not deliver us into Saul's hands.

One day, I received an unexpected visitor—Jonathan! Somehow, Jonathan had learned where I was hiding and came to encourage me in the Lord.

"Listen," Jonathan said, "don't be afraid. I still believe that God will protect you, and my father won't lay a hand on you. David, I truly believe in my heart that someday you will be king over Israel, and I will be second in command next to you!"

I was deeply moved by Jonathan's words. "Oh, my friend Jonathan, there's nothing I would love more than for you to rule by my side!"

"I'm sure even my father Saul knows this," Jonathan continued. "He may not want to admit it, but in his heart, I'm sure he knows that God has anointed you as the next king of Israel. And, as much as I hate to say it, I think he knows that God has lifted His anointing from him."

With tears in my eyes, I took Jonathan's hand, and we both knelt and renewed our covenant before the Lord. Then Jonathan returned home, but I remained at Horesh.

However, while Jonathan was with me, some of the Ziphites found out and went to Saul at Gibeah, informing him that I was hiding among their tribes in the strongholds at Horesh.

"If it pleases your Majesty," they said, "come down whenever you wish, and we'll help deliver David into your hands."

Saul replied, "May the Lord bless you for watching out for me. Now, go and gather more information. Find out where David usually goes and who is with him. Many times I've thought I had him trapped, but he is crafty and always manages to escape. Once your people find his hiding places, tell no one else and report back to me. Then, with you by my side, we will track him down and destroy him! Remember, tell no one else... I'm not sure whom I can trust anymore."

The Ziphites agreed and became spies for Saul. They went to Ziph ahead of Saul, searching for me and my men. But once more, the Spirit of the Lord revealed their plans to me, and the Lord protected us.

Constantly being on the run, always hiding, and endlessly searching for new places to hide began to take a toll on me and my men. One night, unable to sleep, I cried out to the Lord in frustration. Once again, the Lord encouraged me:

"How long wilt Thou forget me, O Lord? Forever?
How long wilt Thou hide Thy face from me?
How long shall I take counsel in my soul, having sorrow in my heart
daily?
How long shall mine enemy be exalted over me?

"Consider and hear me, O Lord my God:
Lighten mine eyes, lest I sleep the sleep of death; lest mine enemy
say, I have prevailed against him; and those that trouble me rejoice
when I am moved.
But I have trusted in Thy mercy; my heart shall rejoice in Thy
salvation.
I will sing unto the Lord, because He hath dealt bountifully with
me."
(Psalm 13 KJV)

After encouraging myself in the Lord, I went down to a place called The Rock and stayed in the Desert of Maon. When Saul's spies reported my location, he once again set out in pursuit.

This time, as Saul was making his way along one side of a mountain, he didn't realize that my men and I were on the other side, hurrying to escape. But we were trapped. Once more, I cried out to the Lord, and once more, the Lord answered.

As Saul and his forces were closing in on us, a messenger came running up to Saul, shouting, "King Saul, come quickly! The Philistines are raiding the land!"

Once more, God intervened on my behalf.

"You have got to be kidding me!" Saul exploded. "David is nearby... I can feel it. And now you're telling me I must leave to fight the Philistines?"

"I'm so sorry," the servant replied, trembling, "but if you and your army don't come right now, the Philistines will surely destroy us and take our women and children!"

Frustrated, Saul broke off his pursuit and led his men to fight the Philistines. That's why we call this place Sela Hammahlekoth, which means "the rock of parting."

Breathing a sigh of relief and giving thanks to God, I went from there to the strongholds of En Gedi. But with Saul constantly tracking me down, I began to wonder if there was a traitor among us.

As we made our way to En Gedi, I began to sing a new psalm:

> "Blessed is he that considereth the poor: the Lord will deliver him in time of trouble.
> The Lord will preserve him, and keep him alive; and he shall be blessed upon the earth: and Thou wilt not deliver him unto the will of his enemies.
> The Lord will strengthen him upon the bed of languishing: Thou wilt make all his bed in his sickness.
>
> "I said, Lord, be merciful unto me: heal my soul; for I have sinned against Thee.
> Mine enemies speak evil of me, when shall he die, and his name perish?
> And if he come to see me, he speaketh vanity: his heart gathereth iniquity to itself; when he goeth abroad, he telleth it.
>
> "All that hate me whisper together against me: against me do they devise my hurt.
> An evil disease, say they, cleaveth fast unto him: and now that he lieth he shall rise up no more.
> Yea, mine own familiar friend, in whom I trusted, which did eat of my bread, hath lifted up his heel against me.
>
> "But Thou, O Lord, be merciful unto me, and raise me up, that I may requite them.
> By this I know that Thou favourest me, because mine enemy doth not triumph over me.
> And as for me, Thou upholdest me in mine integrity, and settest me before Thy face forever.
> Blessed be the Lord God of Israel from everlasting, and to everlasting.
> Amen, and Amen."
> (Psalm 41 KJV)

THE CAVE

After defeating the Philistines, Saul once again resumed his pursuit of me.

"Where is he now?" Saul demanded.

"We've heard he's near the Desert of En Gedi, in a place called the Crags of the Wild Goats," one of his spies informed him.

Gathering three thousand able young men, Saul set out to find me and my men.

I can't believe he's tracked me down again, I thought, frustration surging through me. "Can't I find even a moment's rest without him hunting me?" I grumbled to no one in particular.

"Come on," one of my men said, breaking into my thoughts. "We found a cave nearby where we can hide."

As we huddled in the recesses of the cave, I was once again overwhelmed by my situation. Here I was, hiding like a fugitive. I should be home with my wife, not cowering in this cold, damp cave. I didn't ask for this. I never planned or schemed to take the kingdom from Saul. Yet here I was, reduced to hiding like a lowly animal. So once more, I did the only thing I could—I bowed my head, and my men silently joined me as I prayed. A holy hush fell over us:

> *"Be merciful unto me, O God, be merciful unto me: for my soul trusteth in Thee: yea, in the shadow of Thy wings will I make my refuge, until these calamities be overpast.*
>
> *"I will cry unto God most high; unto God that performeth all things for me.*
> *He shall send from heaven, and save me from the reproach of him that would swallow me up.*

God shall send forth His mercy and His truth.

"My soul is among lions: and I lie even among them that are set on fire, even the sons of men, whose teeth are spears and arrows, and their tongue a sharp sword.
Be Thou exalted, O God, above the heavens; let Thy glory be above all the earth.

"They have prepared a net for my steps; my soul is bowed down: they have digged a pit before me, into the midst whereof they are fallen themselves.

"My heart is fixed, O God, my heart is fixed: I will sing and give praise.
Awake up, my glory; awake, psaltery and harp: I myself will awake early.

"I will praise Thee, O Lord, among the people: I will sing unto Thee among the nations.
For Thy mercy is great unto the heavens, and Thy truth unto the clouds.

"Be Thou exalted, O God, above the heavens: let Thy glory be above all the earth."
(Psalm 57 KJV)

When I finished praying, the only sound in the cave was the drip of water echoing in the silence. It was as if no one wanted to disturb the sacred atmosphere that had filled the dark, cold cave.

Finally, one of my men broke the stillness with a whisper, *"Everyone be quiet—it sounds like Saul is making his way to the entrance of this very cave!"*

Sure enough, to our amazement, Saul entered the very cave where we were hiding and squatted down to relieve himself. He had no idea we were there.

Excitement tinged the voice of one of my men as he whispered in my ear, *"This is the day the Lord spoke of when He said, 'I will give your enemy into your hands for you to deal with as you wish.'"*

Sensing my hesitation, another of my men urged, *"Kill him, David! Kill him now! After all he's done to you, he deserves it! Do it!"*

Slowly and carefully, I crept up behind Saul, making sure not to make a sound. I carefully cut off a corner of his robe without him noticing.

Immediately, I was struck with guilt for what I had done. I quietly made my way back to my men.

"Why didn't you kill him?" one of them whispered urgently, struggling to keep his voice down. *"You had the perfect opportunity! Did you chicken out?"*

I held a finger to my lips, signaling for silence until Saul left the cave.

Once Saul exited, I turned to my men and said, "I know you may not understand this, but the Lord forbid that I should do such a thing to my master, the Lord's anointed, or lay my hand on him; for he is the anointed of the Lord."

"The Lord's anointed? You're the one who's anointed! That's why we're following you!" one of my men challenged.

Raising my hand to quell the argument, I rebuked them sharply. "Listen to me. I want to make this absolutely clear: under no circumstances are any of you to take Saul's life. Do you understand?"

They nodded, but I remained unconvinced.

After Saul had moved some distance from the cave, I stepped out and called loudly, "My lord the king!"

Startled, Saul turned to see me bowing with my face to the ground.

Lifting my head, I called out, "Why do you listen to those who say, 'David is bent on harming you'? Today, you've seen with your own eyes how the Lord delivered you into my hands in this cave. Some of my men urged me to kill you, but I spared you; I said, 'I will not lay my hand on my lord, because he is the Lord's anointed.' Look, my father, at this piece of your robe I hold in my hand! I cut off the corner of your robe but did not kill you. See that there is nothing in my hand to indicate that I am guilty of wrongdoing or rebellion. I have not wronged you, yet you are hunting me down to take my life. May the Lord judge between you and me. May the Lord avenge the wrongs you have done to me, but my hand will not touch you. As the old saying goes, 'From evildoers come evil deeds,' so my hand will not touch you. Who is the king of Israel pursuing? A dead dog? A flea? May the Lord be our judge and decide between us. May He consider my cause and uphold it; may He vindicate me by delivering me from your hand."

When I finished speaking, Saul stood in silence, absorbing my words.

Finally, he responded, "Is that your voice, David my son?"

"Yes, Father, it is," I replied.

Saul fell to his knees, weeping loudly. "You are more righteous than I," he shouted. "You have treated me well, but I have treated you badly. You have just now told me of the good you did to me; the Lord delivered me into your hands, but you did not kill me. When a man finds his enemy, does he let him get away unharmed? May the Lord reward you well for how you treated me today. I know that you will surely be king and that the kingdom of Israel will be established in your hands. Now swear to me by the Lord that you will not kill off my descendants or wipe out my name from my father's family."

I was deeply moved by Saul's emotional response and surprised to hear him acknowledge that I would one day replace him as king.

"I give you my word, O King, that I will not lay a hand on any of your descendants!" I shouted, my voice thick with emotion.

Slowly, Saul rose to his feet, motioned to his men to follow, and walked away from me and my men.

After years of running from Saul, at that moment, I finally felt a glimmer of hope that I might find some peace.

DAVID AND ABIGAIL

"**S**amuel has died," the man told me.

"What?" I responded, my voice filled with disbelief.

"The great prophet Samuel has died," the man repeated softly.

My heart ached at the news. I turned away, seeking solitude to grieve in private.

I recalled vividly the day Samuel anointed me with oil. It was Samuel who introduced me to the Spirit of the Lord—a day that changed my life forever. I had always admired Samuel for his bravery in confronting Saul about his failings, risking his own life to do what was right in the eyes of the Lord. And now... this great man of God was gone.

Who would be the next prophet bold enough to speak truth to the king? What was I to do, where was I to go?

With Saul's recent promise that he would no longer pursue me to kill me, I decided it was safe to return to Jerusalem and mourn Samuel's passing.

It was a moving tribute to a great man of God. All of Israel assembled to mourn Samuel. After a week of mourning, we buried him at his home in Ramah. Then I went down into the Desert of Paran.

Meanwhile, in Maon, a wealthy man named Nabal was shearing his sheep. His wife, Abigail, was known for her intelligence and beauty, while her husband was infamous for his surliness, meanness, and arrogance.

While I was in the wilderness, I learned that Nabal was nearby. I sent ten young men to him with the message, "Go up to Nabal at Carmel and greet him in my name. Say to him: 'Long life to you! Good health to you and your household! And good health to all that is yours! I hear it is sheep-shearing time. When your shepherds were with us, we did not mistreat them, and nothing of theirs went missing. Ask your own servants, and they will tell you. Therefore, be favorable toward my men, since we come at a festive time. Please give your servants and your son David whatever food and supplies you can find.'"

My men delivered the message and waited.

Nabal's response was scathing. "Who is this David? Who is this son of Jesse? Am I supposed to know who he is? There are many servants breaking away from their masters these days. Why should I take my bread and water and the meat I have prepared for my shearers and give it to men who come from who knows where?"

My men were taken aback but said nothing in return. They reported Nabal's words to David precisely.

"Are you sure that's what he said?" I asked, shocked.

"That is exactly what he said," the servant confirmed.

The other servants nodded in agreement.

My anger flared. "After all we have done for him... and this is how he responds?" I shouted. "Strap on your swords!"

"Are we going to avenge your honor?" one of my men asked.

"Yes! We will show this man what happens when my name is slandered!"

About four hundred armed men accompanied me while two hundred stayed with the supplies.

As we made our way I grumbled to myself, *"After everything we've done— protecting his property in the wilderness so that nothing went missing— how dare he disrespect me? He has paid me back evil for good. May God deal with me severely if I leave even one male of his alive by morning!"*

My men encouraged my rage. "That's right, David... let's go get him! We'll show him a thing or two!"

One of Nabal's servants, fearing the consequences, ran to Abigail and told her, "David sent messengers from the wilderness to greet our master, but Nabal insulted them. These men were good to us—they did not mistreat us, and nothing went missing while we were with them. They were a protective wall around us. Please, consider what you can do because disaster seems imminent, and Nabal is too wicked to listen to reason."

Abigail's face turned pale with fear. "Thank you for informing me!"

She acted swiftly. She prepared two hundred loaves of bread, two skins of wine, five dressed sheep, sixty pounds of roasted grain, a hundred cakes of raisins, and two hundred cakes of pressed figs, loading them onto donkeys.

She instructed her servants, "Go on ahead; I'll follow you."

"Aren't you going to tell Nabal what you're doing?" one of the servants asked.

"No, it's best he doesn't find out," Abigail replied. "Let's keep this our little secret!"

Abigail rode her donkey swiftly. As she approached a mountain ravine, she saw me and my men descending toward Nabal's location. She dismounted and bowed before me, her face to the ground. "Pardon your servant, my lord, and let me speak. Hear what your servant has to say."

I motioned for her to continue.

"Please disregard that wicked man Nabal. His name means 'fool,' and folly goes with him. I did not see the men my lord sent. But as surely as the Lord your God lives, and as you live, since the Lord has kept you from bloodshed and from avenging yourself, may your enemies be vanquished. Let this gift be given to the men who follow you. Forgive your servant's presumption. The Lord your God will make a lasting dynasty for you because you fight the Lord's battles, and no wrongdoing will be found in you. Even though someone is pursuing you to take your life, your life will be bound securely in the bundle of the living by the Lord, while your enemies will be hurled away like stones from a sling. When the Lord has fulfilled every good thing He promised you and appointed you ruler over Israel, you won't have the burden of needless bloodshed or personal vengeance. And when you are successful, remember your servant."

I was touched and somewhat amused by Abigail's passionate plea, especially since she was very beautiful.

"Praise be to the Lord, the God of Israel," I responded, "who has sent you to meet me today. May you be blessed for your good judgment and for keeping me from bloodshed and vengeance. As surely as the Lord, the God of Israel, lives, if you had not come quickly, not one male of Nabal's would have been left alive by morning."

"Thank you… thank you… thank you!" Abigail responded. "You truly are a great man!"

I accepted Abigail's peace offering and told her, "Go home in peace. I have heard your words and granted your request."

When Abigail returned home, Nabal was in high spirits, having enjoyed an exquisite banquet and was very drunk. She decided not to tell him about her actions until the next morning.

The following day, when Nabal was sober, Abigail informed him of what had transpired. She was prepared for anger but found him staring at her, unresponsive. She soon realized something was wrong—his heart was not beating normally. He lay there, unable to move, like a stone. Abigail realized he had suffered a major stroke.

Despite her efforts, Nabal died ten days later after the Lord struck him.

Upon hearing of Nabal's death, I said, "Praise be to the Lord, who has upheld my cause against Nabal for treating me with contempt. He has kept me from wrongdoing and brought Nabal's deeds upon his own head."

Then I considered Abigail. "What will become of her? Where will she go?"

I decided to ask her if she would become my wife.

I sent word to Abigail, asking if she was interested in marrying me.

My servants went to Carmel, found Abigail, and relayed my message.

She bowed down and said, "I am your servant, ready to serve you and wash the feet of your servants."

Abigail promptly mounted her donkey and accompanied by five female servants, she returned with my messengers and became my wife.

In the meantime, Saul had given his daughter Michal, my wife, to another man.

SAUL'S SPEAR AND WATER JUG

"What do you think?" one of my men asked me.

"Unfortunately, I think Saul has reverted to his old, jealous self and is once again in a fit of rage against me," I replied.

I had hoped that after our encounter in the cave where I cut off a corner of his robe and he offered such a profound apology, he had experienced a change of heart. But it seemed that was not the case.

Some Ziphites had gone to Saul at Gibeah and informed him, "King Saul, if you're still searching for David, he's hiding on the hill of Hakilah, which faces Jeshimon."

Saul could have dismissed their information, but instead he eagerly responded, "Oh yes, I'm still looking for him! I can't wait to kill him!"

So, Saul set out for the Desert of Ziph with three thousand Israelite troops to search for me.

"What are we going to do?" one of my men asked.

"I think we need to determine exactly how many men Saul has with him and where they are camped," I answered.

"Sounds like a plan," the man responded.

We set out to locate Saul's camp. Once again, the Spirit of the Lord guided me to where Saul and Abner son of Ner, the commander of the army, were resting.

I asked Ahimelek the Hittite and Abishai son of Zeruiah, Joab's brother, "Who will go down into Saul's camp with me?"

"I'll go with you," said Abishai.

Quietly, we made our way through the sleeping soldiers until we found Saul, sound asleep with his spear stuck in the ground near his head.

Abishai whispered excitedly, *"Today God has delivered your enemy into your hands. Let me pin him to the ground with one thrust of the spear; I won't have to strike him twice."*

I replied, "No. Absolutely not! Don't destroy him! Who can lay a hand on the Lord's anointed and be guiltless? As surely as the Lord lives, the Lord Himself will strike him, or his time will come and he will die, or he will go into battle and perish. But the Lord forbid that I should be the one to lay a hand on the Lord's anointed. Instead, let's just take his spear and water jug that are near his head, and let's go."

As quietly as we came, we left, taking Saul's spear and water jug. No one saw or knew about it, nor did anyone wake up. They were all deeply asleep, for the Spirit of the Lord had put them into a deep slumber. Once more, the Spirit of the Lord was with me.

When we crossed over to the other side and stood on top of the hill some distance away, I called out loudly to the army and to Abner son of Ner, "Hey Abner, can you hear me? Are you going to answer me?"

Startled by my shout, Abner jumped to his feet and called out, "Who is it that calls out to the king?"

I shouted back, "You're a man, aren't you? Who is like you in Israel? Isn't it your job to guard the king's life? Someone, meaning me, came to destroy your lord the king. What you've done is not good. As surely as the Lord lives, you and your men must die because you did not guard your master, the Lord's anointed. Look around you. Where are the king's spear and water jug that were near his head? You can't find them, can you? That's because I have them!"

Saul, awakened by the shouting, recognized my voice and leaped to his feet, crying out, "Is that your voice, David my son?"

I replied, "Yes, it is, my lord the king."

Then I added, "Why is my lord pursuing his servant again? What have I done, and what wrong am I guilty of? Now let my lord the king listen to my words. If the Lord has incited you against me, may He accept an offering. If, however, people have done it, may they be cursed before the Lord! They have driven me from my share in the Lord's inheritance and have said, 'Go, serve other gods.' Do not let my blood fall to the ground far from the presence of the Lord. The king of Israel has come out to look for a flea—like one hunts a partridge in the mountains."

Saul listened intently and finally responded, "David, you are right. I have sinned. Please come back to me, David, my son. Because you considered my life precious today, I give you my word that I will not try to harm you again. Surely, I have acted foolishly and have been terribly wrong."

Holding up Saul's spear, I answered, "Here is your spear; let one of your young men come and get it. The Lord rewards everyone for their righteousness and faithfulness. Saul, as you can see, once more the Lord delivered you into my hands, but I would not lay a hand on the Lord's anointed. As surely as I valued your life today, may the Lord value my life and deliver me from all trouble."

With his voice trembling with emotion, Saul replied, "May you be blessed, David my son; you will do great things and surely triumph."

We then parted ways, and Saul returned home.

As I made my way back, I thought to myself, *One day I will surely be destroyed by Saul. The best course of action is to escape to the land of the Philistines. Then Saul will give up searching for me in Israel, and I will slip out of his grasp.*

Once more, I sat down and began to write:

Preserve me, O God: for in Thee do I put my trust.

O my soul, thou hast said unto the Lord,
Thou art my Lord: my goodness extendeth not to Thee; but to the saints that are in the earth, and to the excellent, in whom is all my delight.

Their sorrows shall be multiplied that hasten after another god: their drink offerings of blood will I not offer, nor take up their names into my lips.

The Lord is the portion of mine inheritance and of my cup: Thou maintainest my lot.

The lines are fallen unto me in pleasant places; yea, I have a goodly heritage.

I will bless the Lord, who hath given me counsel: my reins also instruct me in the night seasons.
I have set the Lord always before me: because He is at my right hand, I shall not be moved.

Therefore my heart is glad, and my glory rejoiceth: my flesh also shall rest in hope.
For Thou wilt not leave my soul in hell; neither wilt Thou suffer Thine Holy One to see corruption.
Thou wilt shew me the path of life: in Thy presence is fulness of joy; at Thy right hand there are pleasures for evermore.
(Psalm 16 KJV)

"Where do you want to go now?" one of my commanders asked. "You don't really believe Saul is going to give up trying to kill you, do you?"

"I don't know where to go," I replied. "And no, in my heart of hearts I know the hatred and jealousy Saul has for me are greater than any short-term regret he may feel for seeking to kill me."

"We are running out of places to hide," the commander stated. "What do you think about us returning to Gath?"

"Well," I said, "who knows? Maybe if we surrender ourselves to the king of Gath, he will show us mercy."

So, that is what we did. My six hundred men and I went to Achish son of Maok, king of Gath.

Yes, we decided to return to the land of the Philistines once again. This time, I brought my two wives, Ahinoam of Jezreel and Abigail of Carmel, and each of my men brought their families. We threw ourselves on the mercy of King Achish.

DAVID IN GATH

When we arrived at Gath, I went to King Achish to seek his favor. As I was brought before him, he looked at me with a squint. "Have we met before?" he asked.

I knew it was time to come clean. "Yes," I said, my voice betraying my hesitation. "However, the last time we met, I was slobbering all over myself like a madman."

King Achish stared at me for a few seconds, and I wasn't sure how he would react to my deception. Suddenly, he threw back his head and began laughing hysterically. "That WAS you!" he exclaimed. "You were the one scratching at the door and acting crazy!"

I grinned back at him. "Yes, O King, that was indeed me."

I was relieved to see him taking the news so well.

"And now, here you are again, seeking refuge in our country?"

I bowed and said, "Yes, O King. If I may find favor in your eyes, please assign me a place in one of the country towns where I might reside. I do not expect to live in the royal city with you."

Once again, the Spirit of the Lord was with me, granting me favor and softening King Achish's heart.

"Yes," King Achish replied. "Who knows, perhaps I can spare a few things for the great warrior David."

That day, Achish granted me and my men the area of Ziklag, which has belonged to the kings of Judah ever since. In this strange turn of events, I lived in peace for the first time in many years in Philistine territory for a year and four months.

During our time there, as a sign of goodwill, my men and I raided the enemies of the Philistines—the Geshurites, the Girzites, and the Amalekites. Whenever we attacked an area, we left no man or woman alive but took sheep, cattle, donkeys, camels, and clothes. Each time we returned to King Achish, we presented him with the spoils of war.

When Achish asked, "Where did you go raiding today?" I would reply, "Against the Negev of Judah," or "Against the Negev of Jerahmeel," or "Against the Negev of the Kenites."

The towns of Negev were part of Israel, so Achish was pleased to think we were attacking Israel. This became our practice while we lived in Philistine territory.

Over time, Achish grew to trust me more and more, convincing himself, "Surely David has become so frustrated with his own people, the Israelites, that he will be my servant for the rest of his life."

However, not long after, the Philistines gathered their forces for battle against the armies of Israel. As we had done in previous battles, my men and I prepared to join the Philistine army. But one of the Philistine commanders approached King Achish with concern. "What about these Hebrews?" he asked.

Achish replied, "I understand your concern. I know this is David, who was once a high-ranking officer in the Israelite army. However, he and his men have been with us for over a year, and from the day he left Saul until now, I have found no reason to suspect him. I trust him to do what he says he will do."

Despite Achish's confidence, some Philistine commanders remained wary of me and my men. They grew angry with Achish, saying, "Listen, you may trust him, but we don't! Send him and his men back. You cannot allow them to go with us into battle. How can you be sure that once he faces the Israelites, he won't turn against us? What better way for him to regain King Saul's favor than by betraying us? Don't you remember the songs the Israelite women sang: 'Saul has slain his thousands, and David his tens of thousands'?"

King Achish pondered their concerns and eventually called me for a meeting. "David," he said, "as surely as the Lord lives, you have been reliable, and I would be pleased to have you serve with me in battle today. Honestly, from the day you came to me until now, I have found no fault in you. However, my men don't approve of you. They are worried about your true allegiance, and I understand their concerns. Please, do me a favor and turn back in peace; do nothing to displease the leaders of my army."

At first, I resisted. "But what have I done? What have you found against me from the day I came to you until now? Why can't I go and fight against the enemies of my lord the king?"

Achish answered, "I know you have been as pleasing in my eyes as an angel of God; nevertheless, the Philistine commanders have said, 'He must not go up with us into battle.' I must listen to their concerns. Please, just get up early with your servants and leave in the morning as soon as it is light."

Understanding his position, my men and I left early the next morning and returned to Philistine territory while the Philistines went up to Jezreel to fight King Saul and the Israelites without us.

DAVID RETURNS TO ZIKLAG

I didn't realize it at the time, but when King Achish sent us back to Ziklag, it was the hand of the Lord at work. Upon our return, we were horrified to discover that the Amalekites had raided Ziklag, burning everything to the ground. Fortunately, they hadn't killed any of our women and children; instead, they had taken them captive—all of them, both young and old.

My men and I were devastated. We wept aloud until we had no strength left to weep. My two wives and my children were among those who had been captured. To my shock, I overheard some of my men blaming me, even threatening to stone me to death!

Not knowing what else to do, I turned to the Lord. In the midst of this great tragedy, I found strength in my God. I gathered myself together and went to Abiathar the priest, the son of Ahimelech. "Bring me the ephod," I said.

Abiathar brought it to me, and I fell on my face, inquiring of the Lord, *"Shall I pursue this raiding party? Will I overtake them?"*

"Pursue them," the Lord answered. *"You will certainly overtake them and succeed in the rescue."*

That was all I needed to hear.

"Let's go!" I shouted to my six hundred men. Fortunately, they abandoned any thoughts of taking my life and rallied behind me. However, when we reached the Besor Valley, two hundred of them were too exhausted to cross. Understanding their plight, I told them to stay and regain their strength. The remaining four hundred of us continued the pursuit.

During our pursuit, we came across an Egyptian in a field. He was certain we were going to kill him, but instead, we showed him mercy. I sat down next to him and asked, "Who do you belong to? Where do you come from? And when was the last time you had anything to eat or drink?"

"I am an Egyptian," the man replied, still trembling with fear. "I am the slave of an Amalekite. My master abandoned me and left me to die when I became ill three days ago. We raided the Negev of the Kerethites, the territory belonging to Judah, and the Negev of Caleb. And we also burned Ziklag."

"Did you say you were at Ziklag?" I asked.

"Yes," he replied. "We took all the women and children."

"Are they unharmed?" I asked.

"Oh yes, they are well."

"Can you lead me to this raiding party?" I asked.

"I can," he answered, "but swear to me before God that you will not kill me or hand me over to my master, and I will take you to them."

"I swear," I answered.

As promised, the Egyptian led us to where the Amalekites were. They were scattered across the countryside, eating, drinking, and reveling in the great amount of plunder they had taken from the land of the Philistines and from our village.

"What do you want to do?" one of my commanders asked.

"Look at them," I replied. "They are drinking themselves into a stupor. Let's wait a bit longer, and soon they won't be able to stand, let alone defend themselves."

At dusk, when most of them had passed out, we attacked. None escaped except four hundred young men who fled on camels. We didn't lose a single man.

Just as the Lord had promised, we recovered everything the Amalekites had taken, including our wives and children. Nothing was missing—young or old, boy or girl, plunder, and everything else they had taken. We brought back everything the enemy had stolen! It was a joyous time. We gathered all the flocks and herds, and my men drove them ahead of the other livestock, singing, *"This is David's plunder... this is David's plunder."*

It was hard to believe that just a few days earlier, some of these same men were threatening to stone me to death!

When we returned to the two hundred men who had been too exhausted to continue and were left behind at the Besor Valley, they ran out to meet us, overwhelmed with joy that their wives and children were safe.

However, I overheard some of my men who had fought beginning to complain.

"Because they didn't go out with us, we're not going to share with them the plunder we recovered. They can have their wives and children, but that's all."

I stood up and shouted, "No, my brothers, you must not do that with what the Lord has given us. The Lord has protected us and delivered into our hands the raiding party that came against us. The share of the men who stayed with the supplies is to be the same as that of him who went down to the battle. All will share alike."

Reluctantly, they agreed. From that day forward, I made it a statute and ordinance in Israel that all spoils of battle would be shared equally.

When we reached Ziklag, I decided to send some of the plunder to the elders of Judah, who were still loyal to me, and to those in all the other places where my men and I had roamed. "Here is a gift for you from the plunder of the Lord's enemies," I wrote.

As I reflected on what had just happened, I realized that God had His hand on me once again. Had King Achish allowed me and my men to go with him to fight the Israelites, we would have returned to Ziklag too late to rescue our wives and children from the Amalekites.

Once more, I put pen to paper:

Hear me when I call, O God of my righteousness: Thou hast enlarged me when I was in distress; have mercy upon me, and hear my prayer.

O ye sons of men, how long will ye turn my glory into shame? How long will ye love vanity, and seek after leasing? But know that the Lord hath set apart him that is godly for Himself: the Lord will hear when I call unto Him.

Stand in awe, and sin not: commune with your own heart upon your bed, and be still. Offer the sacrifices of righteousness, and put your trust in the Lord.

There be many that say, Who will shew us any good?
Lord, lift Thou up the light of Thy countenance upon us.
Thou hast put gladness in my heart, more than in the time that
their corn and their wine increased.
I will both lay me down in peace, and sleep: for Thou, Lord, only
makest me dwell in safety.
(Psalm 4, KJV)

SAUL AND THE WITCH

When Saul first became king and sought to follow God's will, he expelled all the mediums and spiritists from the land. However, after the Lord's anointing left him and the prophet Samuel died, Saul grew lax in obeying God's commandments concerning mediums and witches.

When the Philistines set up camp at Shunem, Saul gathered all Israel and made camp at Gilboa. Upon seeing the size of the Philistine army, terror filled Saul's heart. He prayed and inquired of the Lord, but the Lord did not answer him—neither by dreams nor through the prophets.

In desperation, Saul quietly turned to one of his attendants and said, "I need you to do me a favor. Find me a woman who is a medium, so I may go and inquire of her."

The attendant hesitated, unsure if Saul was testing him. "Why do you ask?" he replied.

"To be honest, I'm desperate for answers, and God is not responding to my prayers."

"But are you sure you want to consult with a witch?" the attendant challenged.

"Do you know of any or not?" Saul responded, his irritation clear.

"I've heard there may still be one in Endor," the servant said.

That night, Saul disguised himself and quietly made his way to the woman. The tent she occupied was dark, with incense burning.

"Hello?" Saul said softly, disguising his voice.

"Who is there?"

"Never mind who I am. I just need you to consult a spirit for me," he said.

"What makes you think I can consult with spirits?"

"You are known among those who speak in the dark. I have money—just bring up the one I name."

The woman, still wary, replied, "Listen, I don't know who you are, but surely you know that King Saul has expelled all the mediums and spiritists from the land. Are you trying to set a trap?"

"Oh no," Saul swore to her, "as surely as the Lord lives, I promise you that you will not be punished for this. I will tell no one."

Reluctantly, the woman asked, "Okay, who is it you want me to bring up for you?"

"Bring up Samuel," he said.

"The prophet Samuel?"

"Yes, the prophet Samuel!"

The woman began chanting her incantations. As she did, a spirit appeared before her. Suddenly, she realized the truth and screamed in terror, "I know who you are! You are King Saul! Why have you deceived me?"

Saul replied, "Okay... okay... so you figured it out. Yes, I am the king, but you don't have to be afraid. Just tell me, what do you see?"

Still unsure, the woman softly replied, "I see a ghostly figure coming up out of the earth."

"Seriously? What does he look like?" Saul asked, squinting to see if he could catch a glimpse.

"I see an old man wearing a robe," she said, describing the man and his robe.

"Oh my," Saul exclaimed, "it really is Samuel."

Trembling with fear, Saul bowed down, prostrating himself with his face to the ground.

The spirit of Samuel then spoke to Saul, "Why have you disturbed me by bringing me up?"

"I am in great distress," Saul replied, his voice shaking. "Everything is falling apart. The Philistines are fighting against me, and God has departed from me. Though I pray, God no longer answers me, either by prophets or by dreams. In my desperation, I have called on you to tell me what to do."

With disgust in his voice, the spirit of Samuel replied, "So, you only consult with me now because the Lord has departed from you and become your enemy? The Lord has done what He foretold through me. The Lord has torn the kingdom from your hands and given it to David, because you did not obey the Lord or carry out His wrath against the Amalekites. Now, concerning tomorrow, the Lord will deliver both Israel and you into the hands of the Philistines. You and your sons will be with me tomorrow, and the Lord will give the army of Israel into the hands of the Philistines."

Realizing that Samuel was foretelling his and his sons' deaths, Saul looked up from where he lay prostrate, filled with terror.

"No… no… no…" he muttered repeatedly as the spirit of Samuel departed.

After some time, one of his servants urged Saul, "King Saul, you need to get up and eat something."

Saul refused.

Finally, the medium knelt beside Saul and said, "Listen, I did what you asked. I risked my life to raise the spirit of Samuel. Now please listen to me—let us give you some food so you may eat and have the strength to go on your way."

Saul still refused, saying, "No, I will not eat."

The men who accompanied Saul joined the woman in urging him to eat. Reluctantly, he finally listened, rising from the ground to sit with his face between his knees, rocking back and forth, utterly distraught.

"I have a fattened calf," the medium said. "Wait here while I butcher it."

Saul was so overcome with distress that he could not move.

After butchering the calf, the woman took some flour, kneaded it, and baked bread without yeast. She then set the food before Saul and his men. Saul finally ate with his men.

To the woman's great relief, as soon as they finished eating, they left.

THE DEATH OF SAUL AND JONATHAN

After hearing the spirit of Samuel foretell the kingdom being torn from his hands and the death of his sons, King Saul was gripped with fear and fled from the Philistines. However, the Philistines relentlessly pursued him and his sons, and as the spirit of Samuel had predicted, they killed Jonathan, Abinadab, and Malki-Shua.

Seeing his sons dead, Saul lost the will to fight. The battle intensified around him, and when the Philistine archers closed in, they struck him with several arrows. Mortally wounded, Saul turned to his armor-bearer and pleaded, "Quickly, draw your sword and run me through, or these uncircumcised Philistines will come, kill me, and abuse my body. Please, don't let that happen!"

But the armor-bearer, terrified, refused. So, Saul drew his own sword. With a look of deep remorse, he cast his eyes to the heavens and thrust himself onto the blade. As he lay dying, thoughts of his life flooded his mind, filling him with regret.

Thus ended the reign of Saul as king of Israel—disgraced and defeated.

When the armor-bearer saw that Saul was dead, he too fell on his sword and died alongside him. So, on that same day, Saul, his three sons, his armor-bearer, and many of his men perished together.

When the Israelites living in the valley and those across the Jordan saw that the army had fled and that Saul and his sons were dead, they abandoned their towns and fled as quickly as they could. The Philistines then moved in and occupied their cities.

It was a very sorrowful day for the nation of Israel.

The following day, as the Philistines stripped the dead, they found the bodies of Saul and his three sons on Mount Gilboa. They brutally cut off Saul's head, stripped him of his armor, and sent messengers throughout the land of the Philistines to proclaim the news of Saul's death in the temples of their idols and among their people. They placed his armor in the temple of the Ashtoreths and fastened his body to the wall of Beth Shan as a gruesome display of their victory over Israel.

When the Israelites heard what the Philistines had done to Saul, they gathered some of their valiant men and marched all night to Beth Shan. There, they took down the bodies of Saul and his sons from the wall and brought them to Jabesh, where they burned the flesh from their bodies. Then they buried their bones under a tamarisk tree in Jabesh and fasted for seven days.

DAVID MOURNS FOR SAUL AND JONATHAN

I didn't learn of Saul's death until two days after returning from a battle with the Amalekites. A disheveled man appeared, bowing before me, his clothes torn and covered in dust.

I studied him for a moment before asking, "Where have you come from?"

"I escaped from the Israelite camp," he replied.

"The Israelite camp?" I repeated.

"Yes."

"Please, tell me what happened in the battle," I urged.

"It was terrible," the man said. "Our men fled, and many were killed. King Saul and three of his sons are dead."

"What?" I exclaimed. "King Saul is dead?"

"Yes."

"And three of his sons?"

"Yes."

I hesitated, my heart heavy. "Is his son Jonathan among the dead?"

"Yes," the man confirmed.

"Are you certain? How do you know for sure that King Saul and Jonathan are dead?"

"Well," the young man began, "I happened to be near Mount Gilboa, and I saw King Saul, leaning on his spear, with chariots and horsemen closing in on him. When he saw me, he called out, and I asked, 'What can I do for you?' He asked who I was, and I told him I was an Amalekite."

"You're an Amalekite?" I asked, disbelief creeping into my voice.

"Yes, I am," the man replied.

"What happened next?" I pressed.

"King Saul then asked me to come closer, saying, 'I am mortally wounded. Please take my life!'"

"Did you do it?" I asked, unable to mask my shock.

"Yes. I did as he asked, seeing that his wounds were fatal, and he wouldn't survive much longer."

He didn't notice the rage building in my eyes.

He continued, "I also took the crown from his head and the band from his arm and brought them here to you, my lord."

When my men and I realized Saul and Jonathan were truly dead, we tore our clothes and wept. We mourned and fasted for Saul, Jonathan, the army of the Lord, and the nation of Israel.

After several days of mourning, I summoned the young man who brought the report of their deaths and asked, "Where are you from? Who is your father?"

"I'm the son of an Amalekite," he answered.

My voice thickened as I asked pointedly, "Why weren't you afraid to lift your hand against the Lord's anointed?"

"What?" the young man asked, confused.

I took a step toward him, repeating the question, anger seething in my voice. "Why weren't you afraid to lift your hand against the Lord's anointed?"

At that moment, I didn't know the young man was lying—I didn't know that Saul had fallen on his own sword.

Turning my back on the man, I called out to one of my men, "Go, strike him down!"

Before the young man could declare his innocence, my man struck him with his sword, and the young man fell dead.

I stood over the lifeless body and declared, "Your blood be on your own head. Your own mouth condemned you when you admitted to killing the Lord's anointed."

Then, I turned and walked away from his lifeless body.

My heart was shattered. I mourned deeply for Saul and Jonathan. In my grief, I composed a song and decreed that all the people of Judah must learn its words:

> *A gazelle lies slain on your heights, Israel. How the mighty have fallen!*
>
> *Tell it not in Gath, proclaim it not in the streets of Ashkelon, lest the daughters of the Philistines rejoice, lest the daughters of the uncircumcised celebrate.*
>
> *Mountains of Gilboa, may you have neither dew nor rain, may no showers fall on your terraced fields.*
> *For there the shield of the mighty was despised, the shield of Saul, no longer rubbed with oil.*
> *From the blood of the slain, from the flesh of the mighty, the bow of Jonathan did not turn back, the sword of Saul did not return unsatisfied.*
>
> *Saul and Jonathan—in life, they were loved and admired, and in death, they were not parted.*
> *They were swifter than eagles, they were stronger than lions.*
>
> *Daughters of Israel, weep for Saul, who clothed you in scarlet and finery, who adorned your garments with ornaments of gold.*
>
> *How the mighty have fallen in battle!*
> *Jonathan lies slain on your heights.*
> *I grieve for you, Jonathan my brother; you were very dear to me.*
> *Your love for me was wonderful, more wonderful than that of women.*
>
> *How the mighty have fallen!*
> *The weapons of war have perished!*
> *(2 Samuel 1:19-27 NIV)*

THE CROWN

After mourning the loss of Saul and Jonathan, I wasn't sure what to do next, so I inquired of the Lord. *"What shall I do? Should I go up to one of the towns of Judah?"*

The Lord answered, *"Yes, go up."*

I then asked, *"Where shall I go?"*

"Go to Hebron," the Lord replied.

When I informed my men of our destination, one of them asked, "Why Hebron?"

"The Lord didn't give me a reason," I responded, "but I believe it's because Hebron is where Abraham, Isaac, and Jacob, along with their wives Sarah, Rebekah, and Leah, are buried. Additionally," I continued, "Hebron was part of the land given to the Levites when Joshua led our ancestors into the Promised Land."

So, I took my two wives, Ahinoam and Abigail, our children, and all the men with me, along with their families, and we settled in Hebron and the surrounding towns.

After we were settled, some of the leaders from Judah came and anointed me as king over the tribe of Judah. It was a joyous occasion, and I was filled with gratitude and humility as they placed the crown on my head. I looked over at my wives and children, who were beaming with pride.

However, I was torn. On one hand, I was grateful that I no longer had to constantly flee from Saul and that I was finally becoming king. But on the other hand, I was heartbroken over the deaths of Saul and my best friend Jonathan. I couldn't help but remember the conversation Jonathan and I had about him sitting beside me when I became king.

As I tried to process my feelings, I sat down and penned two psalms:

The Lord reigneth, He is clothed with majesty; the Lord is clothed with strength, wherewith He hath girded Himself: the world also is stablished, that it cannot be moved.
Thy throne is established of old: Thou art from everlasting.

The floods have lifted up, O Lord, the floods have lifted up their voice; the floods lift up their waves.
The Lord on high is mightier than the noise of many waters, yea, than the mighty waves of the sea.

Thy testimonies are very sure: holiness becometh Thine house, O Lord, forever.
(Psalm 93 KJV)

O come, let us sing unto the Lord: let us make a joyful noise to the Rock of our salvation.
Let us come before His presence with thanksgiving, and make a joyful noise unto Him with psalms.
For the Lord is a great God, and a great King above all gods.
In His hand are the deep places of the earth: the strength of the hills is His also.
The sea is His, and He made it: and His hands formed the dry land.

O come, let us worship and bow down: let us kneel before the Lord our maker.
For He is our God; and we are the people of His pasture, and the sheep of His hand.

Today if ye will hear His voice, harden not your heart, as in the provocation, and as in the day of temptation in the wilderness: when your fathers tempted Me, proved Me, and saw My work. Forty years long was I grieved with this generation, and said, It is a people that do err in their heart, and they have not known My ways: unto whom I sware in My wrath that they should not enter into My rest.
(Psalm 95 KJV)

The words of these psalms helped me realize that I was now stepping into my destiny, fulfilling the anointing that Samuel had placed on me so many years ago when I was just a young shepherd boy. The chants of "All hail the king" lifted my spirits.

I could hardly believe it—after fifteen long years of running from Saul, I finally had hope that I might live a normal life with my wives and children.

And now, I would wear the crown of the king!

From holding a harp and sling, hiding in caves, and fleeing for my life, to sitting on the throne with a scepter in my hand—my heart overflowed with gratitude.

In the midst of the celebration, I took a moment to send a message to the men of Jabesh Gilead, who had buried Saul to show my gratitude:

"May the Lord bless you for showing kindness and great respect to Saul and Jonathan by caring for their bodies and burying them. May the Lord show you the same kindness and faithfulness, and I too will show you favor for what you have done. Be strong and brave, for Saul, your master, is dead, and the people of Judah have anointed me as their king."

JUDAH VERSUS ISRAEL

While the men of Judah were anointing me as their king, Abner, Saul's cousin and the top commander in his army, took Ish-Bosheth, Saul's remaining son, and anointed him as king over Gilead, Ashuri, Jezreel, Ephraim, Benjamin, and all of Israel.

Ish-Bosheth was weak, but that didn't bother Abner. In fact, Abner relished the opportunity to run things from behind the scenes.

Fortunately, the tribe of Judah remained loyal to me. One day, Abner was sitting by the pool of Gibeon with some of his men when Joab, one of my commanders, arrived with a group of my men and sat down on the opposite side of the pool. Abner stood up and yelled across, "Hey Joab, why don't we let some of our young men square off against each other?"

Joab jumped to his feet and replied, "Sounds great! How many?"

"Twelve from each side," Abner suggested.

"Sounds good to me," Joab agreed.

The fight quickly turned ugly. My men overwhelmed the men of Israel, thrusting daggers into their sides. Seeing their defeat, Abner fled. However, Asahel, one of my young men known for his speed, began chasing him.

As Asahel was about to catch up, Abner looked back and called, "Is that you, Asahel?"

"It is," Asahel replied.

"Turn aside and take on one of the other young men. If you catch him, you can strip him of his weapons," Abner urged. But Asahel was determined and refused to give up the chase.

Realizing he couldn't outrun Asahel, Abner stopped and faced him.

"Stop chasing me!" he yelled. "I don't want to fight you. If I kill you, how will I face your brother Joab?"

But Asahel wouldn't relent. It was no contest—when Asahel charged, Abner, being the more experienced soldier, sidestepped and thrust the butt of his spear into Asahel's stomach with such force that it came out through his back, killing him instantly.

When Joab and his men reached the site of the fight, they found Asahel's body and were overwhelmed with grief at the violent and savage manner of his death. Quickly, Joab and another man pursued Abner. They chased him all day until the sun began to set.

By then, some of Abner's men had caught up with him, and Joab's men had also arrived. They faced each other on top of a hill. Abner called out to Joab, "I tried to persuade Asahel to stop chasing me, but he refused. What was I supposed to do? Let him kill me? Please, put away your swords and let's call a truce. How many more must die today? Must the sword devour forever? Don't you realize this will end badly? How long before you order your men to stop pursuing their fellow Israelites?"

Joab realized Abner made sense and replied, "As surely as God lives, if you hadn't spoken, my men would have continued pursuing you until morning."

So, Joab blew a trumpet, and all the soldiers halted. At Joab's command, they turned and returned home, no longer pursuing Israel or fighting against them.

Besides Asahel, nineteen of my men were killed. However, my men had killed three hundred and sixty of those with Abner. Joab took Asahel's body and buried him in his father's tomb at Bethlehem. Then Joab and his men marched all night and arrived back at Hebron the next morning.

JUDAH AND ISRAEL UNITED

The conflict between the house of Saul and my house lasted a long time. As my armies grew stronger, the house of Saul's armies grew weaker. Meanwhile, the Lord blessed me and my house immensely. Six sons were born to me and my wives in Hebron: Amnon, Kileab, Absalom, Adonijah, Shephatiah, and Ithream.

As the war between the houses of Saul and David continued, Abner strengthened his position in Saul's house. He became so brazen that he started an affair with Rizpah, one of Saul's concubines. When Ish-Bosheth found out, he confronted Abner, which did not sit well with him.

"How dare you confront me?" Abner shouted at Ish-Bosheth. "Am I a lowly dog's head? Am I on the side of Judah and David? Haven't you seen how loyal I've been to the house of your father Saul and to our family and friends? I could have handed you over to David, but I didn't, out of loyalty to our family! And now you accuse me of being involved with this woman? If you continue this nonsense, may God deal with me ever so severely if I don't do for David what we all know the Lord promised him—to transfer the kingdom from the house of Saul to David and establish David's throne over Israel and Judah from Dan to Beersheba."

His bullying worked. Even though Ish-Bosheth knew the truth about Abner's affair, he was too afraid to say anything further.

However, Abner realized that by sleeping with one of Saul's concubines, his authority might now be questioned, and his power was at risk. So, in a bold move, Abner decided to betray Ish-Bosheth and sent messengers to me to see if I wanted to make a deal.

"I come in the name of Abner," the messenger told me. "Abner said to ask you, 'Whose land is it anyway?' Isn't all the land, including Judah, the land of Israel? He wants to make an agreement with you. If you're willing, he will help you bring all of Israel over to you and unite the kingdom."

I knew that was what the Lord wanted, although I was surprised in the manner it was unfolding.

"Okay," I responded. "Tell him I'll make this agreement, but I have one demand: he must send Michal, Saul's daughter and my first wife, to me."

The demand worked. Ish-Bosheth caved and had Michal taken from her husband Paltiel and given to me.

However, Paltiel, her husband, didn't give up easily. As Michal was being taken away, he followed after her, weeping all the way to Bahurim. When Abner saw him, he shouted, "Paltiel, stop your whining and go back home!" Reluctantly, Paltiel obeyed and turned back.

I almost felt sorry for him. Almost...

Abner then gathered the elders of Israel and reminded them, "For some time, many of you have wanted to make David your king. Now is the time! We all know what the Lord promised David: *'By my servant David, I will rescue my people Israel from the hand of the Philistines and from all their enemies.'*"

The elders of Israel remembered how Samuel had anointed me and knew it was time to make me king over all Israel. Abner then went to the leaders of Judah, shared the plan with them, and came to Hebron to tell me everything that Israel and the whole tribe of Judah wanted to do. When Abner arrived, he brought twenty men with him, and I called for a feast to be prepared for them.

Abner then said to me, "This is a great day. Let me go at once and assemble all of Israel for you, my lord the king, so that they may make a covenant with you, and you may rule over all that your heart desires." I agreed and sent Abner away in peace.

While this was happening, Joab and his men had gone into battle. The battle was a huge success, and they returned with much plunder. However, as they neared the city, one of Joab's servants met him and said, "You'll never guess who's been here and what's taken place while you were gone."

"What happened?" Joab asked.

"While you were in battle, Abner arranged for David to become king of both Israel and Judah!"

"What? How did he manage that?" Joab shouted, clearly disturbed by the news. "Where is Abner now?"

"King David sent him away in peace," the servant replied.

Joab stormed in to see me and demanded, "What have you done? Abner came to you, right? Why did you let him go? Now he's gone! You know what kind of man Abner is. Surely you realize he came to deceive you, to observe your movements and find out everything you're doing, didn't you?"

I wasn't convinced and said so. "I know what kind of person Abner is, but in this situation, he is right. We need to reunite the kingdom, and he is the only person who can do so."

Disappointed, Joab left but decided to send messengers after Abner, telling him I wanted to see him again. They brought Abner back, but I didn't know what Joab was planning behind my back.

When Abner returned to Hebron, Joab took him aside into an inner chamber, as if to speak with him privately on my behalf. There, to avenge the blood of his brother Asahel, Joab quickly stabbed Abner in the stomach, killing him.

When I heard what Joab had done, I was furious and declared, "I and my kingdom are forever innocent before the Lord concerning the blood of Abner, son of Ner. May his blood fall on the head of Joab and his whole family! May Joab's family never be without someone who has a running sore or leprosy, who leans on a crutch, who falls by the sword, or who lacks food."

I then ordered Joab and all his men to tear their clothes, put on sackcloth, and mourn for Abner. And they did. They buried Abner in Hebron, and I wept aloud at his grave. Then I sang this lament:

> "Should Abner have died as the lawless die?
> Your hands were not bound,
> Your feet were not fettered.
> You fell as one falls before the wicked."

All the people mourned Abner's death. They tried to persuade me to eat something before the end of the day, but I refused. As they observed my sincerity and mourning, they were pleased and felt reassured that I had no part in Abner's murder. And I declared to the people, "Don't you realize that a great commander and leader has fallen in Israel today? Even though

I'm the anointed king, I feel weak. These sons of Zeruiah—Joab and his brother—are too strong for me. May the Lord repay the evildoer according to his evil deeds!"

Despite Abner's murder, Israel was united with Judah under my reign. Abner's efforts had not been in vain, and the Lord's promise to me was being fulfilled.

RETURNING THE ARK OF THE COVENANT

After becoming the king over all of Israel I knew the Ark of the Covenant was important, so I decided to bring the Ark back to Jerusalem.

I gathered thirty thousand young men, and we went to Baalah in Judah to bring back the Ark of God, which is called by the name, the name of the Lord Almighty, who is enthroned between the cherubim on the Ark.

However, in my haste to move the Ark I did not consult the ceremonial requirements for handling the Ark. Foolishly, we decided to simply set the Ark of God on a new cart.

Uzzah and Ahio, sons of a man named Abinadab, were guiding the cart, and Ahio was walking in front of it. A large band of Israelites were with me, and we were celebrating with all our might before the Lord, with castanets, harps, lyres, timbrels, sistrums and cymbals. It truly was a joyous occasion.

However, when we crossed the threshing floor of Nakon, the ox that was pulling the cart stumbled, causing the Ark to slip, and Uzzah reached out and took hold of the Ark of God to keep it from falling.

Even though he did so in ignorance, when he touched the Ark, the Lord's anger burned against Uzzah because it was an irreverent act; therefore, God struck him down, and he died right there beside the Ark of God.

I was horrified!

When I saw what happened I did not understand, and I became very angry and afraid and shouted, "How can I bring the ark of the Lord back with me now?"

"So… what do you want us to do with the ark?" one of the men asked.

"I don't know," I responded, still in shock of what had happened.

"Do you want us to leave it at whose ever house that is," the man asked pointing to a house nearby.

"I live there," a man stated, stepping out of the crowd of people that had gathered around.

"What is your name?" I asked.

"I am Obed-Edom."

"Where are you from?"

"I am from the tribe of Levi of the line of Korah, and I would be honored to keep the ark at my house."

I didn't find out until later, but as a Levite, Obed-Edom knew the danger of touching the Ark. But he also knew the blessing that came with the possession of the Ark.

I returned to Jerusalem and Obed-Edom very carefully moved the Ark into his house.

Immediately God began blessing the household of Obed-Edom. His health and the health of his family improved. His crops grew at an amazing rate. His cattle produced more milk than ever. All of the female animals got pregnant. Without doubt, God's hand of blessing was resting on all that Obed-Edom possessed!

God's hand of blessing on him was so pronounced word began to spread among all the people.

About three months later, one of my servants came to me and said, "O King, I just thought you might want to know, the Lord has blessed the household of Obed-Edom and everything he has, because of the Ark of God."

"Seriously?" I responded.

"Oh yes! Everything he possesses is being blessed at an unusual rate. Everyone is saying it's because God is blessing him for taking care of the Ark."

"Bring me a Levite. I want to know everything there is to know about the Ark!" I demanded.

When the Levite was brought to me, I asked him about the proper way to move the Ark.

"Did you notice the four rings on the outside of the Ark?" the Levite asked.

"Yes."

"Those are where long poles are to be inserted, and the Ark is to be carried on the shoulders of someone from the tribe of Levi."

"And if we carry it that way, I don't have to worry about God striking someone else dead?" I asked.

"No," the Levite responded.

"What about sacrifices?" I asked. "Should we offer up sacrifices to the Lord when we move the Ark?"

"There is no requirement in the law, but it would show great respect if you were to do so."

So, I went once more to bring up the Ark of God from the house of Obed-Edom to Jerusalem, again gathering worshippers and musicians, playing their castanets, harps, lyres, timbrels, sistrums and cymbals.

However, this time we carried the Ark with long poles inserted through the rings on the side of the Ark, the way God instructed.

When those who were carrying the Ark of the Lord had taken six steps, I commanded them to stop. There we sacrificed a bull and a fattened calf.

With us handling the Ark the right way I was so overwhelmed with the presence of the Lord and the fact that the Ark was being returned to Jerusalem, I began dancing before the Lord with all my might. In my exuberance I removed all of my clothes until the only thing I was wearing was my linen ephod.

I danced before the Lord in a manner I had never danced before. I didn't care how I looked. I danced with all my might, disregarding how I may appear!

As the Ark of the Lord was entering the city, my wife Michal was watching the celebration from a window. When she saw me leaping and dancing before the Lord, wearing only my under garments, she got very angry.

We brought the Ark of the Lord and carefully placed it inside a tent that I had prepared for it, and we sacrificed many more burnt offerings and fellowship offerings before the Lord.

After we had finished sacrificing the burnt offerings and fellowship offerings, I gathered all the people around and blessed them in the name of the Lord Almighty. Then I gave a loaf of bread, a cake of dates and a cake of raisins to each person in the whole crowd, both men and women.

And all the people went to their homes, rejoicing and singing praises to the Lord Almighty.

When I returned home, I was still rejoicing. However, Michal came out to meet me and said angrily, "How dare you act like that? I can't believe you disgraced yourself and the position as the king of Israel by dancing the way you did, half-naked in full view of those slave girls! What a vulgar thing to do!"

However, I was not ashamed, and replied, "Listen, I wasn't dancing for those slave girls, I was dancing for the Lord. He is the one who chose me rather than your father or anyone from his house when He appointed me as king over Israel. I don't care what you think, or anyone else thinks, I will celebrate before the Lord. And if you think that was embarrassing, you haven't seen anything yet! I will become even more undignified! I don't mind being humiliated in my own eyes. But, concerning those slave girls you spoke of, I will be held in honor in their eyes."

Michal turned and stormed away.

And she bore no children to the day of her death.

Not detoured by Michal's outburst, I sat down and began to write:

> *Let God arise, let His enemies be scattered: let them also that hate Him flee before Him.*
> *As smoke is driven away, so drive them away: as wax melteth before the fire, so let the wicked perish at the presence of God.*
> *But let the righteous be glad; let them rejoice before God: yea, let them exceedingly rejoice.*
>
> *Sing unto God, sing praises to His name: extol Him that rideth upon the heavens by His name Jah, and rejoice before Him.*
>
> *A Father of the fatherless, and a Judge of the widows, is God in His holy habitation.*

God setteth the solitary in families: He bringeth out those which are bound with chains: but the rebellious dwell in a dry land.

O God, when Thou wentest forth before Thy people, when Thou didst march through the wilderness; the earth shook, the heavens also dropped at the presence of God: even Sinai itself was moved at the presence of God, the God of Israel.
Thou, O God, didst send a plentiful rain, whereby Thou didst confirm Thine inheritance, when it was weary.
Thy congregation hath dwelt therein: Thou, O God, hast prepared of Thy goodness for the poor.

The Lord gave the word: great was the company of those that published it.
Kings of armies did flee apace: and she that tarried at home divided the spoil.
Though ye have lien among the pots, yet shall ye be as the wings of a dove covered with silver, and her feathers with yellow gold.
When the Almighty scattered kings in it, it was white as snow in Salmon.

The hill of God is as the hill of Bashan; an high hill as the hill of Bashan.
Why leap ye, ye high hills? This is the hill which God desireth to dwell in; yea, the Lord will dwell in it forever.

The chariots of God are twenty thousand, even thousands of angels: the Lord is among them, as in Sinai, in the holy place.
Thou hast ascended on high, Thou hast led captivity captive: Thou hast received gifts for men; yea, for the rebellious also, that the Lord God might dwell among them.

Blessed be the Lord, who daily loadeth us with benefits, even the God of our salvation.

He that is our God is the God of salvation; and unto God the Lord belong the issues from death.

But God shall wound the head of His enemies, and the hairy scalp of such an one as goeth on still in his trespasses.
The Lord said, I will bring again from Bashan, I will bring My people again from the depths of the sea: that thy foot may be dipped in the blood of thine enemies, and the tongue of thy dogs in the same.

They have seen Thy goings, O God; even the goings of my God, my King, in the sanctuary.
The singers went before, the players on instruments followed after; among them were the damsels playing with timbrels.
Bless ye God in the congregations, even the Lord, from the fountain of Israel.
There is little Benjamin with their ruler, the princes of Judah and their council, the princes of Zebulun, and the princes of Naphtali.

Thy God hath commanded thy strength: strengthen, O God, that which Thou hast wrought for us.
Because of Thy temple at Jerusalem shall kings bring presents unto Thee.
Rebuke the company of spearmen, the multitude of the bulls, with the calves of the people, till every one submit himself with pieces of silver: scatter Thou the people that delight in war.
Princes shall come out of Egypt; Ethiopia shall soon stretch out her hands unto God.

Sing unto God, ye kingdoms of the earth; O sing praises unto the Lord; to Him that rideth upon the heavens of heavens, which were of old!
Lo, He doth send out His voice, and that a mighty voice.
Ascribe ye strength unto God: His excellency is over Israel, and His strength is in the clouds.
O God, thou art terrible out of Thy holy places: the God of Israel is He that giveth strength and power unto His people.

Blessed be God. (Psalm 68 KJV)

DAVID LONGS TO BUILD A TEMPLE

After I was settled in the palace and the Ark of the Covenant was back in Jerusalem, the Lord granted me rest from all my enemies. It was a time of peace across the land, with the Lord's blessing upon the nation.

One day, I spoke to the prophet Nathan. "Here I am, living in a palace of cedar, while the Ark of God remains in a tent. It doesn't seem right. What do you think?"

Nathan replied, "Do whatever you have in mind, for the Lord is with you."

That night, however, the word of the Lord came to Nathan, instructing him: "Go and tell David, 'This is what the Lord says: Are you the one to build me a house to dwell in? I have not dwelt in a house from the day I brought Israel out of Egypt to this day. I have been moving with a tent as my dwelling. Did I ever ask the leaders of Israel, 'Why have you not built me a house of cedar?'

"Tell David, *'The Lord Almighty says: I took you from the pasture, from tending the flock, and appointed you ruler over Israel. I have been with you wherever you went, and I have defeated your enemies. Now, I will make your name great, like the names of the greatest men on earth. I will provide a home for my people Israel, where they will no longer be oppressed. The Lord declares that He will establish a house for you. When your days are over, I will raise up your offspring to succeed you, and I will establish his kingdom. He will build a house for My Name, and I will establish his throne forever. I will be his Father, and he will be My son. When he does wrong, I will punish him, but My love will never be taken away from him. Your house and kingdom will endure forever before Me; your throne will be established forever.'"*

Nathan relayed the Lord's words to me, and I went before the Lord in prayer:

"Who am I, Sovereign Lord, that You have brought me this far? You have spoken of my house's future. For the sake of Your word and Your will, You have done this great thing. How great You are, Sovereign Lord! There is no one like You, no God but You. You have redeemed Israel to be Your people forever. Now, Lord, fulfill Your promise concerning my house so that Your name will be great forever. The Lord Almighty is God over Israel, and the house of Your servant David will endure forever. Please bless the house of Your servant, Sovereign Lord, as You have promised."

Though I was not chosen to build the temple, the Lord blessed me greatly. He gave me victory over the Philistines, Moabites, and many other enemies. Wherever I went, the Lord gave me success, and I reigned over Israel, striving to do what was just and right for all the people.

DAVID MEETS MEPHIBOSHETH

One day, while practicing with my bow, I thought of Jonathan, my dearest friend. I asked my servant, "Is there anyone left of Saul's house to whom I can show kindness for Jonathan's sake?"

"There is a servant of Saul named Ziba," he replied. "She would know."

I found Ziba and asked, "Is there anyone left from Saul's family to whom I can show God's kindness?"

"Yes," she said. "Jonathan's son, Mephibosheth, is still alive, but he is lame in both feet."

I asked where he was, and Ziba explained that he lived in Lo Debar. She also told me that Mephibosheth had become lame when his nurse, fleeing with him after hearing of Saul and Jonathan's deaths, fell, injuring him.

I sent for Mephibosheth.

When he arrived, he bowed before me, filled with fear. "Don't be afraid," I said. "I will show you kindness for your father Jonathan's sake. I will restore to you all of Saul's land, and you will always have a seat at my table."

Overcome with emotion, Mephibosheth responded, "Who am I, that you should notice a dead dog like me?"

I reassured him, "You are the grandson of a king and the son of my closest friend."

Mephibosheth was amazed to learn about my friendship with his father. We spoke for hours, and when I learned he had a young son, Mika, I invited his entire family to live in Jerusalem. It brought me great joy to honor the covenant I had made with Jonathan.

DAVID SHOWS MORE KINDNESS

"Your Majesty," one of my servants said, bowing before me, "I thought you should know that King Nahash of the Ammonites has passed away. He was kind to you when you were fleeing from King Saul."

"Yes," I replied, "I remember how he showed me great kindness."

"I noticed what you did for Jonathan's son," the servant continued. "Is there anything you would like me to do in honor of King Nahash?"

"Oh, yes, that's a wonderful idea," I responded. "Just as I showed kindness to Mephibosheth, I wish to extend the same to Nahash's son. His name is Hanun, if I recall correctly. Please send a delegation to express my condolences for his father's passing."

However, when the delegation arrived, the commanders of the Ammonite army grew suspicious.

"We don't believe King David is sincere," they told Hanun. "We suspect David sent this delegation to spy on our land."

My envoys tried to assure them of my good intentions, but Hanun sided with his commanders.

"What should we do with these men?" one of the commanders asked.

"Seize them!" Hanun ordered. "Let's humiliate David. Shave off half their beards and cut off their garments at the waist, exposing their buttocks!"

The commanders laughed in delight at the thought of shaming my men in such a way.

When I heard of the disgraceful treatment my men endured, I sent word for them to stay in Jericho until their beards had grown back.

Realizing they had angered me, Hanun and the Ammonites began preparing for my response. They hired twenty thousand Aramean soldiers, along with the king of Maakah and a thousand of his men, and twelve thousand more from Tob.

To defend my men's honor, I dispatched Joab with the entire army of Israel's finest warriors. The Ammonites formed battle lines at the entrance to their city gates, while the Arameans, along with the troops from Maakah and Tob, positioned themselves in the open countryside.

But they were no match for the might of Joab and the armies of Israel.

Seeing the enemy positioned both in front and behind him, Joab carefully selected his best troops and deployed them against the Arameans. He placed the rest under the command of his brother, Abishai, to face the Ammonites.

Joab said to Abishai, "If the Arameans are too strong for me, come to my aid. And if the Ammonites are too strong for you, I will come to help you. Be strong and fight bravely for our people and for the cities of our God. The Lord will do what seems best to Him."

When Joab and his troops advanced against the Arameans, the enemy was struck with fear and fled before them. Upon hearing of the Aramean retreat, the Ammonites also fled from Abishai, seeking refuge within their city.

Instead of laying siege to the city, Joab returned to Jerusalem to seek my counsel.

Meanwhile, the Arameans regrouped beyond the Euphrates River. When I learned of this, I ordered Joab to muster all the armies of Israel and cross the Jordan to confront them.

The Arameans were utterly defeated by Israel that day. We destroyed seven hundred of their charioteers and forty thousand of their foot soldiers. It was a resounding victory, and word of Israel's triumph quickly spread throughout the land.

Hearing of this, the surrounding kings hastened to send envoys to make peace with Israel.

DAVID AND BATHSHEBA

It was springtime, the season when kings go off to war. I knew I should have been with my men, yet I made the gravest mistake of my life—I stayed behind in Jerusalem while I sent Joab and the Israelite army off to fight without me.

It all began innocently enough...

One evening, being unable to sleep while my men were in battle, I got up from bed. I was walking on the roof of my palace when I noticed a beautiful woman bathing. I should have looked away, but instead, I lingered, allowing lust to take root in my heart.

The temptation of Bathsheba, the woman I had seen, overwhelmed me. I sent a messenger to inquire about her. The messenger returned, informing me, "Her name is Bathsheba, daughter of Eliam, and wife of Uriah the Hittite."

"Eliam and Uriah?" I asked in disbelief. "Both of them are among my thirty mighty men, loyal and brave warriors!"

Everything in me urged me to turn away, to leave this woman alone. Yet, I foolishly let my desires overpower my better judgment. I learned that both her father and husband were away, fighting for me on the battlefield. I should have stopped there—but instead, I gave a fateful order: "Bring her to me."

The messenger hesitated. "Are you certain, King David?"

I wish now that I could turn back time. But back then, my heart was blinded by lust.

"Do as you're told!" I commanded.

Bathsheba was brought to me, and what should never have happened, happened. I abused my power and convinced her to lie with me. How I wish I had followed Moses' example, choosing the ways of God rather than fleeting, sinful pleasures.

Afterwards, my conscience was tormented, but I hoped to conceal my sin. I thought the matter was over—until Bathsheba sent word: *"I am pregnant."*

Panic gripped me. I knew I should confess, but I chose instead to hide my wrongdoing. I called for Uriah, Bathsheba's husband, to be brought back from the battlefield. When he arrived, I feigned concern for the war and his well-being, encouraging him to go home to his wife. I even sent a gift with him, hoping he would sleep with her and everyone would believe the child to be his.

But Uriah didn't go home. My messenger reported, "He's sleeping outside the palace doors."

Frustrated, I summoned Uriah again. "Why didn't you go home?" I asked.

He replied, "How could I go home to eat, drink, and be with my wife when the Ark of God, Israel, and Judah are living in tents, and my commander and fellow soldiers are in the field? As surely as you live, I cannot do such a thing."

Desperate, I invited him to dine with me, supplying him with food and drink, hoping to lower his guard. But even drunk, Uriah refused to go home. He slept outside the palace once more.

My plan was failing, and I knew my sin would be exposed unless I took more drastic measures. In desperation, I wrote a letter to Joab: *"Put Uriah in the front lines where the fighting is fiercest, then withdraw the troops so he will be struck down and killed."*

I handed the letter to Uriah himself, sealing his fate with his own hands.

Joab obeyed. Uriah was killed in battle.

When the report came back, listing the casualties, Joab's message included, "Uriah the Hittite is dead."

I tried to hide my relief as I dismissed the messenger, telling him to encourage Joab: "Don't let this upset you; the sword devours one as well as another. Press the attack and destroy the city."

The guilt weighed on me heavily. What had I done?

Bathsheba mourned her husband's death, as was custom, but shortly after, I brought her to the palace, and she became my wife. She bore me a son, and for months we kept our affair hidden from the public.

But though we tried to hide it, what we had done greatly displeased the Lord.

DAVID REPENTS

I was miserable—overwhelmed by the guilt and shame of what I had done. It followed me relentlessly. I couldn't sleep, couldn't pray. No more psalms, no more music, no more songs. I hid my harp on a shelf, out of sight.

Yet, even in my misery, I clung to the deceptive voice in my head, whispering that it would be alright—just keep it hidden, and no one will ever know.

I recalled the words of Moses, when the children of Gad and Reuben sought to settle on the wrong side of the Jordan River rather than fight with the rest of Israel. Moses warned them, *"If you do not do this, you will have sinned against the Lord; and be sure your sin will find you out."* (based on Numbers 32:23)

But I had convinced myself that even though many knew of my sin, they would help me keep it hidden. Little did I know, the Lord was speaking to Nathan, the prophet.

I remember the knock at the door that day.

"O King," a servant said, "Nathan the prophet is here to see you."

"Send him in," I replied.

Nathan entered, and after exchanging pleasantries, he said, "I need your counsel."

Relieved that it wasn't about me, I listened. "Of course," I said. "How can I help?"

Nathan began, "There were two men, one rich and one poor. The rich man had many sheep and cattle, while the poor man had nothing but one small ewe lamb, which he had raised like a daughter. The lamb ate from his plate, drank from his cup, and slept in his arms."

My heart softened. Recalling my years as a shepherd, I knew well the affection one could have for a lamb.

Nathan continued, "One day, a guest visited the rich man, but instead of the rich man taking one of his own flock to prepare a meal, he seized the poor man's only lamb and served it to his guest for dinner."

My blood boiled. I leaped to my feet, furious. "As surely as the Lord lives," I shouted, "the man who did this must die! He must pay for that lamb four times over!"

Nathan stood and walked toward me until we were face to face. His voice thundered, *"You are that man!"*

It hit me like a hammer! My sin was exposed! I was that man!

Nathan continued, "This is what the Lord says: *'I anointed you king over Israel. I delivered you from Saul. I gave you your master's house, wives, and the kingdoms of Israel and Judah. And if that had been too little, I would have given you even more. Why, then, have you despised My word? You struck down Uriah the Hittite with the sword and took his wife to be your own. Now the sword will never depart from your house.'"*

I collapsed under the weight of his words, for every one of them were true. God had blessed me beyond measure, and I had taken it all for granted.

Nathan's judgment continued: *"'Out of your household, calamity will come upon you. Before your eyes, your wives will be given to another, and he will lie with them publicly. What you did in secret, I will do in broad daylight before all Israel.'"*

The enormity of my sin crashed down on me. I fell on my face, weeping. "I have sinned against the Lord," I cried.

Nathan's voice softened. "The Lord has taken away your sin; you are not going to die. But because you have shown utter contempt for Him, the son born to you will die."

I was crushed, my heart shattered.

After Nathan left, the Lord struck the child with illness. I pleaded with God. I fasted, wept, and lay in sackcloth for days, begging for the child's life. My servants urged me to rise and eat, but I refused.

I prayed fervently:

"O Lord, rebuke me not in Thine anger, neither chasten me in Thy hot displeasure.
Have mercy upon me, O Lord; for I am weak: O Lord, heal me; for my bones are vexed.
My soul is also sore vexed: but Thou, O Lord, how long?

"Return, O Lord, deliver my soul: oh save me for Thy mercies' sake.
For in death there is no remembrance of Thee: in the grave who shall give Thee thanks?

"I am weary with my groaning; all the night make I my bed to swim; I water my couch with my tears.
Mine eye is consumed because of grief; it waxeth old because of all mine enemies.

"Depart from me, all ye workers of iniquity; for the Lord hath heard the voice of my weeping.
The Lord hath heard my supplication; the Lord will receive my prayer.
Let all mine enemies be ashamed and sore vexed: let them return and be ashamed suddenly."
(Psalm 6 KJV)

"Have mercy upon me, O God, according to Thy lovingkindness: according unto the multitude of Thy tender mercies blot out my transgressions.
Wash me throughly from mine iniquity, and cleanse me from my sin.

"For I acknowledge my transgressions: and my sin is ever before me.
Against Thee, Thee only, have I sinned, and done this evil in Thy sight: that Thou mightest be justified when Thou speakest, and be clear when Thou judgest.

"Behold, I was shapen in iniquity; and in sin did my mother conceive me.
Behold, Thou desirest truth in the inward parts: and in the hidden part Thou shalt make me to know wisdom.

"Purge me with hyssop, and I shall be clean: wash me, and I shall be whiter than snow.
Make me to hear joy and gladness; that the bones which Thou hast broken may rejoice.
Hide Thy face from my sins, and blot out all mine iniquities.

"Create in me a clean heart, O God; and renew a right spirit within me.
Cast me not away from Thy presence; and take not Thy Holy Spirit from me.

"Restore unto me the joy of Thy salvation; and uphold me with Thy free spirit.
Then will I teach transgressors Thy ways; and sinners shall be converted unto Thee.

"Deliver me from bloodguiltiness, O God, Thou God of my salvation: and my tongue shall sing aloud of Thy righteousness.
O Lord, open Thou my lips; and my mouth shall shew forth Thy praise.
For Thou desirest not sacrifice; else would I give it: Thou delightest not in burnt offering.
The sacrifices of God are a broken spirit: a broken and a contrite heart, O God, Thou wilt not despise.

"Do good in Thy good pleasure unto Zion: build Thou the walls of Jerusalem.
Then shalt Thou be pleased with the sacrifices of righteousness, with burnt offering and whole burnt offering: then shall they offer bullocks upon Thine altar."
(Psalm 51 KJV)

That truly was my prayer, that others who may have failed God the same way I did, would find the same type of repentance and forgiveness! That transgressors would find their way back to the Lord and sinners would turn to God. That was one of the only sources of comfort to me during this time – that others would learn from my mistake!

Seven days later, the child died. My servants hesitated to tell me, fearing I might do something desperate. But I already knew.

"Is the child dead?" I asked quietly.

"Yes," they replied.

I rose, bathed, dressed, and went to the house of the Lord to worship.

For the first time in months, I felt peace. My sin had estranged me from God, and it felt so good to fellowship with Him again.

After worship, I returned home and ate. My servants, baffled, asked, "Why this change? When the child was alive, you fasted and wept, but now that he's dead, you eat."

I explained, "While the child lived, I thought perhaps the Lord would be gracious and spare him. But now that he's gone, fasting cannot bring him back. One day, I will go to him, but he cannot return to me."

The grief between Bathsheba and me was immense. We held each other, weeping for the loss that was caused by our sin. But over time, the Lord began to heal us.

Then, in His grace, He gave us another son—Solomon.

Nathan visited us again, but this time, there was no condemnation. Instead, he smiled warmly and embraced us. "The Lord loves this child," he said. "He is special to God, just as you are."

Relief washed over us. God's mercy had not only forgiven us but blessed us.

Soon after, I returned to battle, leading the army myself. With the Lord's favor restored, we captured the city of Rabbah, and the crown of the Ammonite king was placed on my head—a crown of gold weighing seventy-five pounds, adorned with precious stones. Victory was sweet, but nothing compared to the sweetness of once again walking in the favor of the Lord.

AMNON AND TAMAR

Despite God's favor returning to me, the words I had spoken to Nathan still haunted me: the rich man who took the poor man's lamb would pay fourfold.

Although I knew God had forgiven me, I was also aware that He is just, and that sin carries consequences.

The first consequence of my sin was clear: the death of our child. The second consequence came through my son Amnon.

Unbeknownst to me, my eldest son Amnon, whom I had with Ahinoam, had become obsessed with his half-sister Tamar, the daughter of my wife Maacah. Tamar was stunningly beautiful, like her mother, and Amnon convinced himself that he was in love with her. His obsession was so intense that it made him physically ill.

Tamar, my beloved daughter, was a righteous young woman and a virgin. I was incredibly proud of her. Amnon, on the other hand, had started running around with Jonadab, my nephew—Shimeah's son—a man I had never trusted. Jonadab was cunning and deceitful, and I feared his influence over my son.

Seeing Amnon's constant melancholy mood, Jonadab asked, "Why do you, the king's son, look so haggard every day? What's troubling you?"

Amnon replied, "I'm in love with Tamar, my brother Absalom's sister."

Jonadab, with his sly nature, hatched a plan. "Pretend to be ill," he suggested. "When your father comes to see you, ask him to have Tamar prepare food in your presence, so you can eat from her hand."

Amnon followed Jonadab's advice, and when I visited my son, he requested that Tamar make him some special bread to help his appetite. Wanting to comfort my ailing son, I sent word to Tamar to fulfill his request.

Tamar, eager to help her half-brother, arrived at his house, prepared the bread in his sight, and brought it to him. But when she offered it to him, Amnon refused to eat.

"I don't want anyone else here," Amnon said, asking Tamar to send everyone away.

Trusting her brother, Tamar complied. Alone with him, Amnon revealed his true intentions, grabbing her and saying, "Come to bed with me, my sister."

Tamar recoiled in horror. "No, my brother! Do not commit such a wicked act. Think of the shame it would bring upon me, and the disgrace it would bring to you. Please, speak to our father—he might allow us to marry."

But Amnon ignored her pleas, overpowered her, and raped her.

Afterward, his desire turned to hatred. "Get up and get out!" he shouted, consumed by intense loathing for her.

Tamar, devastated, begged, "No! Sending me away now would be an even greater wrong than what you've already done."

But Amnon called his servant and ordered her to be thrown out and the door bolted behind her.

Overwhelmed, Tamar tore the ornate robe she wore, the special garment given to the virgin daughters of the king. She put ashes on her head, mourning the violation, and wandered the palace weeping.

Her brother Absalom saw her distress and, after she confirmed what had happened, rage filled him. Yet, he said softly, "Be silent for now, my sister. He is your brother. Do not take this to heart."

Tamar, desolate, moved into Absalom's house and lived in sorrow.

ABSALOM'S REVENGE

When I learned what Amnon had done, I was furious. How could my son commit such an atrocity? I also feared Absalom's reaction, knowing his loyalty and deep bond with Tamar.

For two years, Absalom remained silent, neither speaking nor acknowledging Amnon.

But Absalom's rage smoldered beneath the surface. After two years, he invited all his brothers to a sheepshearing celebration. He also invited me, but I declined, sensing unease. Yet when Absalom specifically asked for Amnon to join, I hesitated but eventually consented, thinking perhaps this could be a step toward reconciliation.

My fears were justified. Once Amnon was intoxicated, Absalom ordered his men, "Strike Amnon down."

They followed his command and killed him. Afterward, all of Absalom's men fled.

News reached the palace in a garbled form, claiming all my sons had been killed. Devastated, I tore my clothes in grief. But then Jonadab approached and clarified, "Only Amnon is dead."

Though somewhat relieved, I mourned for Amnon, recognizing Absalom had plotted this since Tamar's rape.

Absalom fled to Geshur, and I was left to grieve for both my sons: one dead, and the other a fugitive.

For three years, Absalom remained in Geshur.

Though I longed to see him, I didn't know how to approach him. Joab, perceiving my heart, devised a plan. He sent a wise woman to me, disguised in mourning, to tell me a tale that mirrored my own situation with Absalom. Her words moved me, and I realized the wisdom in her plea. Confronting her, I discerned Joab's hand behind the scheme.

So, I summoned Joab and said, "Bring back my son Absalom, but he must live in his own house. He is not to see my face."

Joab brought Absalom back to Jerusalem, but for two years Absalom did not see me. Still, word spread of his remarkable appearance—his handsome face and thick, heavy hair.

In time, Absalom sought to meet with me, but when Joab refused his requests, Absalom resorted to burning Joab's fields to gain his attention. When Joab confronted him, Absalom expressed his frustration: "Why am I here in Jerusalem if I cannot see my father? It would be better to have remained in Geshur."

Joab relayed this message to me, and finally, I summoned Absalom.

When he arrived, he bowed before me. Moved with compassion, I embraced him and kissed him, hoping this was the beginning of our reconciliation.

ABSALOM'S REBELLION

In time, as Absalom's wealth and popularity grew, so did his arrogance. It reached the point where he acquired a chariot and horses and appointed fifty men to run ahead of him, shouting his praises.

Then, he began rising early and standing by the roadside leading to the city gate. Whenever someone came with a complaint to present to me for judgment, Absalom would call out, "What town are you from?"

Upon hearing their response, he would say, "I am from one of the tribes of Israel."

Then he would add, "Your claims are valid and just, but there is no representative of the king to hear you. If only I were appointed judge in the land, everyone with a complaint or case could come to me, and I would ensure they received justice without delay."

He was deliberately undermining my authority.

When someone approached him and bowed before him, Absalom would reach out his hand, take hold of them, and kiss them.

Absalom behaved this way toward all the Israelites who came seeking justice from me, and in doing so, he stole the hearts of the people of Israel.

I could see what he was trying to do, and it troubled me, but I hoped and prayed for the best. Our relationship was fragile, and I refused to chastise or confront him.

After four years of this behavior, Absalom came to me one day and said, "Father, please allow me to go to Hebron to fulfill a vow I made to the Lord. While I was living in Geshur, I vowed that if the Lord brought me back to Jerusalem, I would worship Him in Hebron."

Though suspicious, I was pleased by his desire to worship the Lord, so I said, "Go in peace."

But, as I suspected, Absalom was up to no good. Instead of going to Hebron to worship, he sent secret messengers throughout the tribes of Israel, instructing them, "As soon as you hear the sound of the trumpets, proclaim, 'Absalom is king in Hebron!'"

He then recruited two hundred men from Jerusalem to accompany him. Though they were initially unaware of his true intentions, Absalom's charm and charisma quickly won them over. While offering sacrifices, Absalom sent for Ahithophel, one of my top counselors, and somehow convinced him to join his rebellion. This marked a turning point in his conspiracy. With Ahithophel's support, Absalom's followers increased significantly.

I tried to ignore what was happening, hoping Absalom's rebellion would fizzle out. But one day, a messenger came to me with grave news.

"O King, I don't know how to say this except to be direct," he said.

"Speak up!" I demanded.

"The hearts of most of Israel are now with Absalom," he said softly.

"How bad is it?" I asked.

"It's very bad. He has gained a large following."

I knew I should have intervened sooner, but a father always wants to believe the best about his children.

"Do you truly think there are more with Absalom than with me?" I asked.

"I'm afraid so," he replied.

I realized action was necessary. "Go quickly," I ordered, "and tell all my officials to gather at once! If we don't flee Jerusalem immediately, none of us will escape Absalom. We must leave now, or he will overtake us, bring ruin upon us, and put the city to the sword."

My officials responded promptly, "Your servants are ready to do whatever our lord the king commands."

We departed, taking my entire household with us, though I left ten concubines behind to care for the palace. We paused at the edge of the city while all my men marched ahead of us. Among them were the Kerethites, Pelethites, and six hundred Gittites who had accompanied me from Gath.

I turned to one of the Gittites and said, "Why are you coming with us? Wouldn't it be better for you to return and stay with Absalom? You are a foreigner, an exile from your homeland. You've only been in Jerusalem a short time. Why should you wander with us when I don't even know where we're going? Go back, take your people, and may the Lord show you kindness and faithfulness."

But the Gittite replied, "As surely as the Lord lives and as you live, wherever you may go, whether in life or death, there I will be with you."

Moved by his loyalty, I said, "Very well, march on," giving him a warm pat on the shoulder.

And so, the Gittites marched on with us.

As word spread of Absalom's betrayal, it seemed the entire countryside wept as we passed. We marched until we crossed the Kidron Valley.

Once more, the Lord spoke to me through song:

"Truly my soul waiteth upon God: from Him cometh my salvation. He only is my rock and my salvation; He is my defence; I shall not be greatly moved.

"How long will ye imagine mischief against a man? Ye shall be slain all of you: as a bowing wall shall ye be, and as a tottering fence. They only consult to cast him down from his excellency: they delight in lies: they bless with their mouth, but they curse inwardly.

"My soul, wait thou only upon God; for my expectation is from Him. He only is my rock and my salvation: He is my defence; I shall not be moved.
In God is my salvation and my glory: the rock of my strength, and my refuge, is in God.
Trust in Him at all times; ye people, pour out your heart before Him: God is a refuge for us.

"Surely men of low degree are vanity, and men of high degree are a lie: to be laid in the balance, they are altogether lighter than vanity. Trust not in oppression, and become not vain in robbery: if riches increase, set not your heart upon them.

"God hath spoken once; twice have I heard this; that power belongeth unto God.

Also unto Thee, O Lord, belongeth mercy: for Thou renderest to every man according to his work."
(Psalm 62 KJV)

Though many had abandoned me, Zadok, my high priest, remained loyal. The Levites, too, stood by me, carrying the Ark of the Covenant. They set it down and offered sacrifices until all the people had left the city.

I then said to Zadok, "Take the Ark of God back to the city. If I find favor in the Lord's eyes, He will bring me back to see it and His dwelling place once more. But if He is displeased with me, I am ready to accept whatever He deems fit."

Zadok, concerned, asked, "Are you sure about this? It sounds like you're thinking of quitting. Are you doubting God's favor?"

I ignored his question. "Please, do as I ask. Return to the city with my blessing. Take your son Ahimaaz and Abiathar's son Jonathan with you. I will wait at the fords in the wilderness until I hear word from you."

Reluctantly, Zadok and Abiathar took the Ark of God back to Jerusalem.

I prayed I was making the right choice:

"Hear my cry, O God; attend unto my prayer.
From the end of the earth will I cry unto Thee, when my heart is overwhelmed: lead me to the rock that is higher than I.

"For Thou hast been a shelter for me, and a strong tower from the enemy.
I will abide in Thy tabernacle forever: I will trust in the covert of Thy wings.

"For Thou, O God, hast heard my vows: Thou hast given me the heritage of those that fear Thy name.
Thou wilt prolong the king's life: and his years as many generations.

He shall abide before God forever: O prepare mercy and truth, which may preserve him.

"So will I sing praise unto Thy name forever, that I may daily perform my vows."
(Psalm 61 KJV)

We continued our journey up to the Mount of Olives, but my heart was breaking. I wept as we went; my head was covered, and I was barefoot. In a show of solidarity, the people with me covered their heads as well as we ascended.

Then, to make matters worse, one of my trusted servants approached me, questioning me about Ahithophel, my former counselor who had betrayed me by joining Absalom. In my distress, I did the only thing that made sense—I prayed.

When we reached the summit, where we used to worship God, Hushai, one of my loyal friends, was there to greet me. His robe was torn, and dust was on his head—a gesture of mourning and solidarity. It was just what I needed.

"Hushai," I said, "you are my dear friend."

Hushai smiled warmly, "I love you too, my king. I would do anything for you."

"I'm glad to hear that," I replied. "Because I have a very important request."

"Say the word, my lord," he responded.

"I want you to return to Jerusalem, go to Absalom, and tell him, 'Your Majesty, I will be your servant; I was your father's servant in the past, but now I will serve you.'"

Hushai raised an eyebrow, "So, you want me to deceive Absalom and become a spy for you?"

"Yes," I said. "But I need you to do this to counter the influence of Ahithophel. He is now advising Absalom, and I need someone on the inside to challenge his counsel."

"Are there others working with you in the city?" Hushai asked.

"Yes. Zadok and Abiathar, my faithful priests, will be there with you. Anything you hear, tell them. They will relay the information through their sons, Ahimaaz and Jonathan, to bring word back to me."

"I'm in," Hushai said firmly.

"May the Lord be with you," I said, embracing him.

Hushai made his way to Jerusalem, arriving just as Absalom was entering the city.

We continued our flight from Absalom. A little beyond the summit, I encountered Ziba, the servant of Mephibosheth, Jonathan's crippled son, whom I had welcomed into my palace.

Ziba brought a string of saddled donkeys laden with bread, cakes of raisins and figs, and a skin of wine.

"Ziba!" I said, surprised. "What is the meaning of this?"

Ziba replied, "You have shown great kindness to my household. These provisions are for your household to ride and eat, and the wine is to refresh those who grow weary in the wilderness."

"Thank you," I said, moved by his generosity. "But where is Mephibosheth?"

"He remains in Jerusalem," Ziba answered. "As you know, he cannot travel, or he would be here with you."

"And how is he faring with all that Absalom is doing?" I asked.

"He hopes that Absalom will eventually restore to him the land you gave him," Ziba said.

"Absalom has taken his land?" I asked, shocked.

"Yes," Ziba confirmed. "It's a sad situation."

"Listen," I said, making a swift decision. "I am still king, even in this dire situation. By my decree, all that belonged to Mephibosheth is now yours until he can reclaim it."

Ziba bowed low, clearly touched by my words. "May I find favor in your eyes, my lord the king."

We spoke for a while, reminiscing about Jonathan, my dear friend, and the time when I welcomed Mephibosheth into my home. As I reflected, I was moved to write:

O God, Thou art my God; early will I seek Thee: my soul thirsteth for Thee, my flesh longeth for Thee in a dry and thirsty land, where no water is; to see Thy power and Thy glory, so as I have seen Thee in the sanctuary.

Because Thy lovingkindness is better than life, my lips shall praise Thee.
Thus will I bless Thee while I live: I will lift up my hands in Thy name.
My soul shall be satisfied as with marrow and fatness; and my mouth shall praise Thee with joyful lips:

When I remember Thee upon my bed, and meditate on Thee in the night watches.
Because Thou hast been my help, therefore in the shadow of Thy wings will I rejoice.
My soul followeth hard after Thee: Thy right hand upholdeth me.

But those that seek my soul, to destroy it, shall go into the lower parts of the earth.
They shall fall by the sword: they shall be a portion for foxes.

But the king shall rejoice in God; every one that sweareth by Him shall glory: but the mouth of them that speak lies shall be stopped.
(Psalm 63, KJV)

Meanwhile, Absalom and his men had made their way to Jerusalem, and Ahithophel, who had betrayed me, was with him.

Then Hushai, my undercover confidant, approached Absalom and said, "Long live the king! Long live the king!"

Absalom responded, "Is this how you show loyalty to your friend, David? If he is your friend, why didn't you go with him?"

Hushai, needing to convince Absalom of his allegiance, replied, "No, the one chosen by the Lord, by the people, and by all of Israel—he is the one I serve, and I will remain with him. Should I not serve the son as I served the father? Just as I was with your father, I will now serve you."

His words convinced Absalom. Fully deceived, Absalom sought Ahithophel's counsel in his bid to overthrow the kingdom. "Give me your advice," Absalom said. "What should we do?"

After a moment of contemplation, Ahithophel replied, "Here is what you should do: sleep with your father's concubines whom he left behind to take care of the palace. When all Israel hears of this, it will make you obnoxious to your father, and the hands of those with you will be strengthened."

Absalom asked, "Will that work?"

Ahithophel confidently responded, "Absolutely. This will demonstrate to the people that you have no regard for your father's legacy, positioning you as a strong, ruthless leader."

That night, they pitched a tent for Absalom on the roof, and he slept with one of my concubines in full view of all Israel.

In those days, the advice Ahithophel gave was regarded as if one had inquired of God Himself. Such was the respect both David and Absalom had for his counsel. His advice was unquestionable.

Thus, when Ahithophel said to Absalom, "Here's my next recommendation: choose twelve thousand men and set out tonight in pursuit of David. Attack him while he is weary and weak, striking him with terror so that his people flee. Then strike down David alone. By doing this, the people will return to you, seeing you as both strong and merciful," the plan seemed good to Absalom and his elders.

However, Absalom, wanting to be cautious, said, "Summon Hushai so I can also hear his counsel on this matter."

When Hushai arrived, Absalom said, "Ahithophel has given us advice. Should we follow it, or do you have another suggestion?"

After listening to Ahithophel's plan, Hushai replied, "I disagree. This time, Ahithophel's advice is flawed. You know your father and his men; they are fighters, as fierce as a bear robbed of her cubs. David is experienced; he won't stay with his troops overnight. Even now, he's probably hidden in a cave. If David were to strike your troops first, the news would spread that Absalom's forces were slaughtered. Then even the bravest soldier would lose heart, for all Israel knows David and his men are seasoned warriors."

Hushai continued, "I advise you to gather all of Israel and lead them into battle yourself. When you find David, attack him with such force that neither he nor his men will survive. If he takes refuge in a city, all Israel will bring ropes and drag the city into the valley until not even a pebble remains."

Absalom and his men were swayed. "We prefer Hushai's advice over Ahithophel's," they said, not realizing that the Lord had determined to frustrate Ahithophel's counsel to bring disaster upon Absalom.

After they decided to follow Hushai's plan, Hushai secretly informed the priests Zadok and Abiathar, who were loyal to me. "Ahithophel advised Absalom to do this, but I have given different counsel. Quickly, send word through your sons, Jonathan and Ahimaaz, to David. Tell him, 'Do not stay at the fords in the wilderness tonight. Cross over immediately, or both the king and all his people will be swallowed up.'"

Jonathan and Ahimaaz set out and made it to En Rogel, where a female servant was to meet them. However, a young man loyal to Absalom spotted them and informed Absalom. Sensing danger, the two messengers fled to Bahurim, where they took refuge in a well. The man of the house covered the opening with a cloth and spread grain over it to disguise their hiding place. When Absalom's men arrived and questioned the woman, she said, "They crossed the brook." Believing her, they searched but found nothing and returned to Jerusalem.

Once the coast was clear, Jonathan and Ahimaaz climbed out of the well and delivered the message to me: "O king, cross the river at once! Ahithophel has advised a plan against you."

I thanked them, saying, "You have done well. May God be with you always."

So, all of us crossed the Jordan by daybreak; no one was left behind.

When Ahithophel realized his advice had been rejected and that I was safe, he saddled his donkey, returned to his hometown, put his house in order, and hanged himself. He was buried in his father's tomb.

ON THE RUN AGAIN

Being on the run from Absalom brought back painful memories of my years fleeing from Saul. While Absalom crossed the Jordan with his men, I sought refuge in Mahanaim. I learned that Absalom had appointed Amasa, my nephew and his cousin, as commander in place of Joab. My heart broke yet again at the number of those I once thought loyal who had betrayed me and sided with Absalom.

However, I found strength in those who were willing to risk their lives to stand by my side. As Absalom's armies camped in Gilead, more young men joined us at Mahanaim. They brought bedding, bowls, and pottery, along with food—wheat, barley, flour, roasted grain, beans, lentils, honey, curds, sheep, and cheese from cow's milk. They said, "We heard you may be exhausted, hungry, and thirsty in the wilderness."

Every time betrayal struck me, it seemed the Lord sent others to lift me up.

Refreshed by these provisions, I mustered the men and appointed commanders over thousands and hundreds. I divided the troops into three groups—one under Joab, one under his brother Abishai, and the third under Ittai the Gittite. I told them, "I will march with you."

But the men objected. "No, David. You must not go with us. If we flee, they won't pursue us—they will come after you. You are worth ten thousand of us. Stay in the city and support us from there."

Though it was hard to accept, they were right. I stayed behind—not out of fear but for the sake of my men. I stood by the gate as they marched out, blessing them with my heart in every step. *This is the day,* I thought, *that my men go into battle against my own son, against those who once were loyal to me.* My heart was torn.

Before they left, I commanded Joab, Abishai, and Ittai, "Please, for my sake, be gentle with Absalom." I made sure all the troops heard me.

The battle took place in the forest of Ephraim. Waiting for news was torture, but the Lord, as always, was with me. My men routed Absalom's forces, and twenty thousand fell that day. The forest claimed more lives than the sword.

As Absalom fled, his mule passed under the thick branches of an oak, and his hair became entangled in the tree. He was left hanging in midair as the mule ran off. One of my men saw this and reported it to Joab, who demanded, "Why didn't you strike him down?" But the man replied, "I would not harm the king's son even for a thousand shekels. We all heard the king's command to spare Absalom."

Joab, ignoring my plea, took three javelins and thrust them into Absalom's heart while he hung helpless. Then ten of Joab's armor-bearers surrounded and struck Absalom until he was dead. They threw his body into a pit and piled stones over it. Absalom's troops fled.

Ahimaaz, son of Zadok, wanted to bring me the news, but Joab sent a Cushite instead. Ahimaaz persisted and eventually was allowed to run after him. He outran the Cushite and arrived first, proclaiming victory, but when I asked about Absalom, he was vague. My heart filled with dread. When the Cushite finally arrived, he said, "May the enemies of my lord the king be like that young man." My heart sank. Absalom was dead.

Overcome with grief, I went to a room above the gate and wept bitterly, crying, "O Absalom, my son! If only I had died instead of you!"

In my grief, I cried out to the Lord:

> *"Why standest Thou afar off, O Lord? Why hidest Thou Thyself in times of trouble?*
>
> *"The wicked in his pride doth persecute the poor: let them be taken in the devices that they have imagined.*
> *For the wicked boasteth of his heart's desire, and blesseth the covetous, whom the Lord abhorreth.*
> *The wicked, through the pride of his countenance, will not seek after God: God is not in all his thoughts.*
> *His ways are always grievous; Thy judgments are far above out of his sight: as for all his enemies, he puffeth at them.*
> *He hath said in his heart, I shall not be moved: for I shall never be in adversity.*

His mouth is full of cursing and deceit and fraud: under his tongue is mischief and vanity.

He sitteth in the lurking places of the villages: in the secret places doth he murder the innocent: his eyes are privily set against the poor.

He lieth in wait secretly as a lion in his den: he lieth in wait to catch the poor: he doth catch the poor, when he draweth him into his net.

He croucheth, and humbleth himself, that the poor may fall by his strong ones.

He hath said in his heart, God hath forgotten: He hideth His face; He will never see it.

"Arise, O Lord; O God, lift up Thine hand: forget not the humble. Wherefore doth the wicked contemn God? He hath said in his heart, Thou wilt not require it.

Thou hast seen it; for Thou beholdest mischief and spite, to requite it with Thy hand: the poor committeth himself unto Thee; Thou art the helper of the fatherless.

Break Thou the arm of the wicked and the evil man: seek out his wickedness till Thou find none.

The Lord is King forever and ever: the heathen are perished out of His land.

Lord, Thou hast heard the desire of the humble: Thou wilt prepare their heart, Thou wilt cause Thine ear to hear:

To judge the fatherless and the oppressed, that the man of the earth may no more oppress."
(Psalm 10 KJV)

Joab heard of my mourning and stayed away, but my sorrow spread through the camp, turning victory into mourning. My soldiers entered the city quietly, as though ashamed. I cried again, "O Absalom, my son!"

Joab eventually came to me, rebuking me. "You have shamed your men today, those who saved your life and the lives of your family. You seem to love those who hate you and hate those who love you. If you do not encourage your men, they will all abandon you by nightfall. It will be worse than all your calamities combined."

I knew he was right, so I gathered myself and sat at the city gate. When the men came before me, I let them know I mourned my son, but I also appreciated their loyalty. They accepted my words with grace.

With Absalom's death came unrest throughout Israel. The tribes debated among themselves—should they bring me back as king, or seek another? I sent word to Zadok and Abiathar, asking the elders of Judah, "Why should you be the last to bring me back to the palace? You are my own flesh and blood. And tell Amasa, 'May God deal with me ever so severely if you are not the commander of my army for life in place of Joab.'"

This message won over the hearts of the men of Judah, and they sent for me. I returned to the palace and prayed:

> *"I was glad when they said unto me, Let us go into the house of the Lord.*
> *Our feet shall stand within thy gates, O Jerusalem.*
> *Jerusalem is builded as a city that is compact together: whither the tribes go up, the tribes of the Lord, unto the testimony of Israel, to give thanks unto the name of the Lord.*
> *For there are set thrones of judgment, the thrones of the house of David.*
> *Pray for the peace of Jerusalem: they shall prosper that love thee.*
> *Peace be within thy walls, and prosperity within thy palaces.*
> *For my brethren and companions' sakes, I will now say, Peace be within thee.*
> *Because of the house of the Lord our God I will seek thy good."*
> (Psalm 122 KJV)

Things were once again turning in my favor, thanks be to Almighty God.

The men of Judah had come to Gilgal to meet me and escort me across the Jordan to Jerusalem. Shimei, son of Gera, the Benjamite from Bahurim, hurried down with the men of Judah to meet me. He was accompanied by a thousand Benjamites, along with Ziba, the steward of Saul's household whom I had blessed, and his fifteen sons and twenty servants. They rushed to the Jordan and crossed at the ford to take control of my household and carry out my wishes.

Yes, things were definitely turning in my favor!

Then Shimei, who had betrayed me, fell prostrate before me and said, "May my lord not hold me guilty. Please do not remember the wrong your servant committed on the day my lord the king left Jerusalem. May the king put it out of his mind. I know I have sinned, but today I am the first from the tribes of Joseph to come down and meet my lord the king."

Abishai interrupted, saying, "King David, this man is a traitor! He should be put to death for cursing the Lord's anointed!"

Though I was glad to see Abishai defending me, I replied, "What does this have to do with you, Abishai? What right do you have to interfere? I am tired of all the killing. I don't want another death in Israel today. I know that I am king over Israel, and I could have those who betrayed me put to death. But today, I choose to show mercy!"

Turning to Shimei, I said, "I promise, you shall not die."

I hoped that showing mercy and forgiveness would bring much-needed healing to the land of Israel.

Then Mephibosheth, Saul's grandson, also came to meet me. He was genuinely concerned for my well-being. I had heard that he had not cared for his feet, trimmed his mustache, or washed his clothes since the day I left.

When he came before me, I asked, "Why didn't you go with me, Mephibosheth? Why did you stay here with Absalom?"

He answered, "My lord the king, as you know, I am lame. I had planned to saddle my donkey and go with you, but Ziba, my servant, betrayed me and slandered me before you. Yet my lord the king is like an angel of God, so do whatever you wish. All of my grandfather's descendants deserved death from you, but you gave me a place among those who eat at your table. For that, I will be forever grateful. What right do I have to make any more appeals to you, O king?"

My heart went out to him, and I said, "Say no more. I order that you and Ziba divide the land."

Mephibosheth bowed and said, "Let him have it all. All I care about is that you have returned home safely."

I was moved by his loyalty.

"No," I responded firmly. "It will be as I have spoken. You and Ziba will divide the land equally."

Mephibosheth bowed once more, full of gratitude, reminding me of the great friendship I had shared with his father, Jonathan.

Another man, Barzillai the Gileadite, also came to meet me when I crossed the Jordan. He was very old, eighty years of age, and had helped me during my time in Mahanaim when I first fled from Absalom. He was a man of great wealth.

I was grateful for his support and said, "Cross over with me and stay in Jerusalem, and I will provide for you as a way to say 'thank you' for your help."

But Barzillai answered, "I appreciate your offer, but how many years do I have left to enjoy it? I am now eighty years old. I can barely tell what is enjoyable or not; I can barely taste food or drink, and I can barely hear the voices of singers. Why should I be a burden to my lord the king? Let me cross over with you for a short distance, then let me return home to die near the tomb of my father and mother. Instead, let my servant Kimham go with you. Do for him whatever you wish."

I agreed. "Very well, I will grant your request. Kimham shall come with me, and I will do for him whatever you desire. Is there anything else you need from me?"

"No," Barzillai replied. "I just want to die in peace, knowing my faithful servant is taken care of."

I kissed him and gave him a long, emotional embrace, reassuring him that I would care for Kimham. Then Barzillai turned and returned to Mahanaim.

That day, I was greatly encouraged by all the people who met me at the Jordan and crossed over with me. Their support made the loss of Absalom easier to bear.

Soon, the men of Israel also came to meet me and said, "Why did our brothers, the men of Judah, steal you away from us and bring you and your household across the Jordan?"

The men of Judah replied, "We did so because the king is our close relative. Why are you angry? Have we taken anything from the king for ourselves? No."

The men of Israel retorted, "We have ten shares in the king; we have a greater claim on him than you! Why treat us with contempt? Weren't we the first to speak of bringing back the king?"

I could see trouble brewing between Israel and Judah, between those who had remained faithful and those who had deserted me.

At that moment, a troublemaker named Sheba, son of Bikri, a Benjamite, sounded the trumpet and declared, "We have no share in David, no part in Jesse's son! Every Israelite, return to your tents! Follow me if you agree!"

To my dismay, all the men of Israel deserted me to follow Sheba. However, the men of Judah stayed with me from the Jordan to Jerusalem.

Upon my return to the palace in Jerusalem, it felt wonderful to be back on the throne.

I took the ten concubines I had left to care for the palace and placed them under guard in a house. Though I provided for them, I had no relations with them. They remained in confinement as widows for the rest of their lives. However, I rewarded them for their loyalty.

Once more, I found myself on my knees before the Lord, reciting a psalm:

> "The earth is the Lord's, and the fulness thereof; the world, and they that dwell therein.
> For He hath founded it upon the seas, and established it upon the floods.
>
> "Who shall ascend into the hill of the Lord? Or who shall stand in His holy place?
> He that hath clean hands, and a pure heart; who hath not lifted up his soul unto vanity, nor sworn deceitfully.
> He shall receive the blessing from the Lord, and righteousness from the God of his salvation.
> This is the generation of them that seek Him, that seek Thy face, O Jacob.
>
> "Lift up your heads, O ye gates; and be ye lift up, ye everlasting doors; and the King of glory shall come in.

Who is this King of glory? The Lord strong and mighty, the Lord mighty in battle.
Lift up your heads, O ye gates; even lift them up, ye everlasting doors; and the King of glory shall come in.
Who is this King of glory? The Lord of hosts, He is the King of glory."
(Psalm 24 KJV)

After tending to the ten women who had maintained the palace in my absence, I decided to give Amasa, my nephew who had betrayed me to Absalom, another chance. I told him, "Go immediately and summon the men of Judah to come to me within three days—and be here yourself."

I waited.

Four days passed with no sign of anyone, and I knew something was wrong.

But I also knew I had to deal with Sheba, the troublemaker, first.

So, I said to Abishai, "Listen, Sheba will cause us more harm than Absalom did. Take some of my men and pursue him, or he'll find fortified cities and escape."

My mighty warriors set out under Abishai's command, marching from Jerusalem to track down Sheba.

While they were near the great rock in Gibeon, Amasa finally appeared.

Joab, dressed in his military tunic, had a dagger strapped to his waist. Knowing Amasa's intentions were not trustworthy, Joab approached him, saying, "How are you, my brother?"

Joab took hold of Amasa's beard with his right hand, as if to greet him with a kiss. Amasa, unsuspecting, did not see the dagger in Joab's left hand. Joab thrust the blade into Amasa's belly with such force that his intestines spilled out onto the ground. Without needing another blow, Amasa fell and died.

Joab and his brother Abishai resumed their pursuit of Sheba.

One of Joab's men stood beside Amasa's body and called out, "Whoever supports Joab and is loyal to David, follow Joab!"

As Joab left Amasa lying in his own blood on the road, the soldiers passing by stopped to stare. Seeing this, the commanders dragged Amasa's body off the road into a field and covered him with a garment to keep the soldiers moving.

Sheba, realizing he was being hunted, passed through all the tribes of Israel until he reached Abel Beth Maakah, where he had gathered a few followers.

Joab's forces caught up with him there.

The city was heavily fortified, so they began building a siege ramp against the walls. As they battered the wall, a wise woman called out from the city, "Listen! Tell Joab to come here so I can speak with him!"

Joab approached and she asked, "Are you Joab?"

"I am," he replied.

"Listen to what I have to say," she said.

"I'm listening," Joab responded.

She continued, "In the past, people said, 'Seek counsel at Abel,' and that would resolve matters. We are a peaceful and faithful city. Why do you seek to destroy it, a city that is a mother in Israel? Why do you want to swallow up the Lord's inheritance?"

"Far be it from me to destroy or swallow up anything!" Joab replied. "That is not my intention. A man named Sheba from the hill country of Ephraim has rebelled against the king and taken refuge here. Hand him over, and we will leave your city."

The woman asked, "What if we throw his head over the wall to you?"

Joab grinned. "You would do that?"

"If it will save the city, yes," she answered.

"Then we have a deal," Joab agreed.

The woman gathered the city's people and shared her plan. Soon after, Sheba's head was tossed over the wall, landing at Joab's feet.

Joab blew the trumpet of retreat, and he and his men withdrew from the city, returning to Jerusalem.

MAKING THINGS RIGHT

It was time to restore order. I appointed Joab over Israel's army; Benaiah, son of Jehoiada, over the Kerethites and Pelethites; Adoniram was in charge of forced labor; Jehoshaphat, son of Ahilud, served as the recorder; Sheva as the secretary; Zadok and Abiathar were priests, and Ira the Jairite became my personal priest.

Yet, for three years there was famine in the land. Once again, I sought the Lord's counsel. The Lord revealed, "It is because of Saul and his blood-stained house; he put the Gibeonites to death."

In the days of Joshua, the Gibeonites, seeing how God's hand was with the Israelites, sought peace with Israel through deceit. Joshua, unaware of their deception, made a covenant with them. Though Joshua later discovered the truth, he allowed them to remain, but made them woodcutters and water carriers as punishment.

Saul, however, violated this covenant without cause, launching a massacre against the Gibeonites. This injustice was the reason for the famine.

I summoned the surviving Gibeonites and asked, "What shall I do for you? How shall I make atonement for Saul's injustice toward your people?"

They replied, "We have no right to demand silver or gold, nor the right to put anyone in Israel to death."

"So, what do you ask of me?" I persisted.

They answered, "Saul tried to destroy us and left us with no place in Israel. Let seven of his male descendants be handed over to us to be killed and exposed before the Lord."

I agreed, sparing Mephibosheth, son of Jonathan, due to my covenant with Jonathan before the Lord. However, I took Armoni and Mephibosheth, the sons of Saul and Rizpah, one of Saul's concubines, as well as five of Saul's grandsons, the sons of Merab. I handed them over to the Gibeonites, who killed them and exposed their bodies on a hill before the Lord. All seven died together at the beginning of the barley harvest.

Later, a servant informed me of Rizpah's actions. She had spread sackcloth on a rock near the bodies of her sons and stayed there, protecting them from birds by day and wild animals by night, until the rains fell from the heavens.

My heart went out to her. I ordered the bones of Saul and Jonathan to be retrieved from Jabesh Gilead, and I brought them to Rizpah. I then buried them, along with the bodies of her sons, in the tomb of Saul's father, Kish, at Zela in Benjamin. After this, God answered prayer on behalf of the land, and the famine was lifted.

DAVID SEEKS TO REPAY THE LORD

*H*ow *can I thank the Lord?* I pondered.

Looking back over my life, I was overwhelmed by God's goodness and blessings. I had wives, children, grandchildren, a beautiful home, wealth, and fortune—all because of God's grace. Yet, when I gazed at the humble tabernacle, the house of the Lord, I felt ashamed. How could the place where God's presence dwelled be so plain?

Though the Lord, through the prophet Nathan, had told me that I would not build the temple because of the bloodshed I had caused, He had not forbidden me from providing the materials.

So, I set to work. I ordered the assembly of skilled laborers. Stonecutters were appointed to prepare dressed stones for God's house. I provided iron for the nails and fittings of the doors, and more bronze than could be weighed. I also provided an abundance of cedar logs.

Knowing Solomon was young and inexperienced, I wanted the temple to be magnificent and splendid in the sight of all nations. I summoned Solomon and charged him with the task of building the house for the Lord.

"My son," I said, "I had it in my heart to build a house for the Name of the Lord, but the word of the Lord came to me, saying, 'You have shed much blood and fought many wars. You will not build a house for My name. Instead, your son, Solomon, a man of peace and rest, will build it. I will grant him rest from all his enemies, and he will reign in peace. He will be My son, and I will be his Father. I will establish his kingdom forever.' Now, my son, may the Lord be with you. Be successful in building the house of the Lord, as He has said. May the Lord grant you discretion and understanding to govern Israel. Be strong and courageous. Follow the law of the Lord, and you will prosper."

I had provided a hundred thousand talents of gold, a million talents of silver, quantities of bronze and iron too vast to measure, and wood and stone. The workers—stonecutters, masons, carpenters, and craftsmen—were countless. 'Now begin the work,' I told Solomon," and may the Lord be with you."

Solomon was humbled by the honor of building the Lord's house. I then commanded all the leaders of Israel to assist him.

Solomon addressed them, saying, "The Lord your God is with you and has granted you rest on every side. Now devote yourselves to seeking Him, and begin to build the sanctuary of the Lord, so that the Ark of the Covenant and the sacred articles of God may be brought into His house."

I was filled with pride as I watched Solomon, confident that the kingdom was in capable hands.

THE FINAL DAYS

Once again, war broke out between the Philistines and Israel. I went down with my men to join the fight, but I was too exhausted to battle. Old age had begun to settle in my bones.

I heard that one of the Philistines, Ishbi-Benob, a descendant of Rapha, was seeking to kill me. His bronze spearhead was said to weigh three and a half pounds, and he boasted of his strength. However, Abishai, my nephew, came to my rescue. Just as I once defeated the giant Goliath, Abishai struck down Ishbi-Benob, slaying him. Needless to say, I was immensely proud of him!

After the battle, when victory was ours, my men came to me and said, "King David, we truly appreciate your heart and courage, but never again will you go out with us to battle, so that the lamp of Israel will not be extinguished."

I knew they spoke the truth. My time on the battlefield had come to an end. I was saddened by this, yet also at peace. I knew it was time to hang up my sword and shield.

In due course, there was another battle with the Philistines at Gob. Sibbekai the Hushathite killed Saph, another giant descended from Rapha. At yet another battle at Gob, Elhanan, son of Jair the Bethlehemite, killed the brother of Goliath, whose spear was as thick as a weaver's rod, nearly two and a half inches thick and almost five feet long.

Then there was a battle at Gath, where a giant of a man appeared. He had six fingers on each hand and six toes on each foot, twenty-four in all. He, too, was descended from Rapha. When he taunted Israel, Jonathan, my nephew, killed him. These four giants—all descendants of Rapha in Gath— fell at the hands of me and my men. My family had become a family of giant slayers!

As I reflected on the many battles I had fought, my victories and defeats, moments of joy and times of sorrow and regret, my heart was full. I felt the love of God so close:

"The transgression of the wicked saith within my heart, that there is no fear of God before his eyes.
For he flattereth himself in his own eyes, until his iniquity be found to be hateful.
The words of his mouth are iniquity and deceit: he hath left off to be wise, and to do good.
He deviseth mischief upon his bed; he setteth himself in a way that is not good; he abhorreth not evil.

"Thy mercy, O Lord, is in the heavens; and Thy faithfulness reacheth unto the clouds.
Thy righteousness is like the great mountains; Thy judgments are a great deep: O Lord, Thou preservest man and beast.
How excellent is Thy lovingkindness, O God!
Therefore the children of men put their trust under the shadow of Thy wings.
They shall be abundantly satisfied with the fatness of Thy house; and Thou shalt make them drink of the river of Thy pleasures.
For with Thee is the fountain of life: in Thy light shall we see light.

"O continue Thy lovingkindness unto them that know Thee; and Thy righteousness to the upright in heart.
Let not the foot of pride come against me, and let not the hand of the wicked remove me.
There are the workers of iniquity fallen: they are cast down, and shall not be able to rise."
(Psalm 36 KJV)

Then I sang to the Lord the words of a song I wrote when the Lord delivered me from the hand of all my enemies and from the hand of Saul:

"The Lord is my rock, my fortress, and my deliverer; My God is my rock, in whom I take refuge,
My shield and the horn of my salvation.
He is my stronghold, my refuge, and my savior—from violent people, You save me. I called to the Lord, Who is worthy of praise, and I have been saved from my enemies.

144

The waves of death swirled about me; the torrents of destruction overwhelmed me.
The cords of the grave coiled around me; the snares of death confronted me.
In my distress, I called to the Lord; I called out to my God.
From His temple, He heard my voice; my cry came to His ears.

The earth trembled and quaked, the foundations of the heavens shook; they trembled because He was angry.
Smoke rose from His nostrils; consuming fire came from His mouth, burning coals blazed out of it.
He parted the heavens and came down; dark clouds were under His feet.
He mounted the cherubim and flew; He soared on the wings of the wind.
He made darkness His canopy around Him—the dark rain clouds of the sky.
Out of the brightness of His presence, bolts of lightning blazed forth.
The Lord thundered from heaven; the voice of the Most High resounded.
He shot His arrows and scattered the enemy, with great bolts of lightning, He routed them.
The valleys of the sea were exposed, and the foundations of the earth were laid bare at the rebuke of the Lord, at the blast of breath from His nostrils.

He reached down from on high and took hold of me; He drew me out of deep waters.
He rescued me from my powerful enemy, from my foes, who were too strong for me.
They confronted me on the day of my disaster, but the Lord was my support.
He brought me out into a spacious place; He rescued me because He delighted in me.

The Lord has dealt with me according to my righteousness; according to the cleanness of my hands, He has rewarded me.

For I have kept the ways of the Lord; I am not guilty of turning from my God.

All His laws are before me; I have not turned away from His decrees.

I have been blameless before Him and have kept myself from sin.

The Lord has rewarded me according to my righteousness, according to my cleanness in His sight.

To the faithful, You show Yourself faithful, to the blameless, You show Yourself blameless, to the pure, You show Yourself pure, but to the devious, You show Yourself shrewd.

You save the humble, but Your eyes are on the haughty to bring them low. You, Lord, are my lamp; the Lord turns my darkness into light.

With Your help, I can advance against a troop; with my God, I can scale a wall.

As for God, His way is perfect: the Lord's word is flawless; He shields all who take refuge in Him.

For who is God besides the Lord?

And who is the Rock except our God?

It is God who arms me with strength and keeps my way secure.

He makes my feet like the feet of a deer; He causes me to stand on the heights.

He trains my hands for battle; my arms can bend a bow of bronze.

You make Your saving help my shield; Your help has made me great.

You provide a broad path for my feet so that my ankles do not give way.

I pursued my enemies and crushed them; I did not turn back until they were destroyed

I crushed them completely, and they could not rise; they fell beneath my feet.

You armed me with strength for battle; You humbled my adversaries before me.

You made my enemies turn their backs in flight, and I destroyed my foes.

They cried for help, but there was no one to save them—to the Lord, but He did not answer.
I beat them as fine as the dust of the earth; I pounded and trampled them like mud in the streets.

You have delivered me from the attacks of the peoples; You have preserved me as the head of nations.
People I did not know now serve me; foreigners cower before me;
As soon as they hear of me, they obey me.
They all lose heart; they come trembling from their strongholds.

The Lord lives! Praise be to my Rock! Exalted be my God, the Rock, my Savior!
He is the God who avenges me, who puts the nations under me, who sets me free from my enemies.
You exalted me above my foes; from a violent man, You rescued me.
Therefore, I will praise You, Lord, among the nations; I will sing the praises of Your name.
He gives His king great victories; He shows unfailing kindness to His anointed, to me and my descendants forever." (2 Samuel 22, NIV)

As I grew older, I found it increasingly difficult to stay warm at night, even with several blankets covering me. One evening, while preparing for bed, some of my attendants brought a young woman to my side.

"King David, this is Abishag," they said. "She is a Shunamite, and she is willing to lie beside you to keep you warm during the night."

I smiled at her, trying to ease any discomfort. "Do not worry," I reassured her, "I have no interest in intimacy."

She burst out laughing, and I wasn't entirely sure how to take it. Still, I was grateful for her presence and the warmth she provided.

One afternoon, as I sat on the porch under the sun, one of my attendants approached me.

"King David, we have a problem," he began.

"What kind of problem?" I asked.

"I hate to say this, but one of your sons is stirring up trouble, declaring that he intends to be the next king."

"Which son?" I inquired.

"Adonijah," he replied. "He's gathered chariots and horses and has fifty men running ahead of him. He's proclaiming, 'I will be king!'"

I couldn't believe what I was hearing. "Who supports him?"

"Joab and Abiathar the priest," he said. "But Zadok the priest, Benaiah, Nathan the prophet, Shimei, Rei, and your special guard remain loyal to you."

I was stunned. "Joab, my military commander, and Abiathar, my priest, have turned against me?"

"Yes," the attendant confirmed. "I know it's hard to believe, but it's true."

Adonijah soon invited all my sons—except for Solomon—to the Stone of Zoheleth near En Rogel to offer sacrifices. Nathan the prophet realized swift action was necessary. He went to Bathsheba, Solomon's mother, and asked, "Have you heard that Adonijah, the son of Haggith, has declared himself king, and our lord David knows nothing of it?"

"No," Bathsheba replied. "I hadn't heard."

"Well, that's the situation," Nathan said. "We must act quickly to protect you and your son Solomon."

"What should we do?" Bathsheba asked.

"You must go to King David and remind him of his oath," Nathan advised. "'My lord, did you not swear to me that Solomon would be king after you? Why then has Adonijah taken the throne?' After you speak to him, I will come and confirm your words."

Following Nathan's plan, Bathsheba came to me as I lay in bed.

"What do you need, my dear wife?" I asked.

She said, "My lord, you swore to me by the Lord your God that our son Solomon would succeed you on the throne. But now Adonijah has become king, and you, my lord, know nothing of it. He has offered sacrifices, gathered the sons of the king, and invited Abiathar the priest and Joab the commander, but not Solomon. The entire nation waits to hear who will be king after you. If you do nothing, once you are gone, Solomon and I will be treated as criminals."

After Bathsheba left, Nathan entered and bowed before me.

"Nathan, what brings you here?" I asked.

He said, "Have you declared that Adonijah will be king? Today, he has offered sacrifices and gathered the commanders of the army, Abiathar the priest, and the king's sons. They are already proclaiming, 'Long live King Adonijah!' But neither Zadok the priest, Benaiah, myself, nor Solomon was invited. Is this your decree?"

I quickly summoned Bathsheba back into my chambers. I declared, "As surely as the Lord lives, who has delivered me from every adversity, today I will fulfill my oath: Solomon, your son, will be king after me, and he will sit on my throne in my place."

Bathsheba bowed low and said, "May my lord King David live forever!"

I called for Zadok the priest, Nathan the prophet, and Benaiah son of Jehoiada.

"Take Solomon," I commanded, "and have him ride my mule to Gihon. There, Zadok the priest and Nathan the prophet will anoint him king over Israel. Blow the trumpet and shout, 'Long live King Solomon!' Then escort him to my throne so he may reign in my place over Israel and Judah."

Benaiah responded with great enthusiasm: "Amen! May the Lord, the God of my lord the king, confirm this. As the Lord has been with you, may He be with Solomon and make his throne even greater!"

So Zadok, Nathan, Benaiah, the Kerethites, and the Pelethites escorted Solomon on my mule to Gihon. Zadok took the horn of oil from the sacred tent and anointed Solomon. The trumpet sounded, and the people shouted, "Long live King Solomon!" The rejoicing was so loud that the earth shook.

Meanwhile, at Adonijah's feast, the sound of the trumpet startled Joab.

"What is the meaning of this uproar?" he asked.

At that moment, Jonathan, son of Abiathar, arrived.

"Come in, you must have good news," Adonijah greeted him.

149

"Not at all," Jonathan replied. "King David has made Solomon king. Solomon has been anointed by Zadok the priest and Nathan the prophet, and he now sits on the royal throne. The city celebrates, and the king himself has blessed Solomon's reign."

Upon hearing this, Adonijah's guests rose in fear and quickly dispersed. In terror, Adonijah fled to the altar and begged for mercy.

When Solomon heard of this, he declared, "If Adonijah proves himself worthy, not a hair on his head will fall. But if he is found guilty of wrongdoing, he will die."

Adonijah was brought before Solomon, bowed low, and was dismissed with the words, "Go home."

With Solomon's kingship secured, I felt the weight of my life finally lift. My strength was fading, and I knew my time was near. My thoughts drifted back to my youth, to the hills of Bethlehem where I had once watched over sheep and sang praises to the Lord. I remembered the day Samuel anointed me, the moment I first felt the Spirit of the Lord. I felt that same Spirit now as I picked up my harp one last time. As I played softly, the Lord gave me a psalm that captured my life's journey:

> "The Lord is my shepherd; I shall not want.
> He maketh me to lie down in green pastures: He leadeth me beside the still waters.
> He restoreth my soul: He leadeth me in the paths of righteousness for His name's sake.
>
> "Yea, though I walk through the valley of the shadow of death, I will fear no evil: for Thou art with me; Thy rod and thy staff they comfort me.
>
> "Thou preparest a table before me in the presence of mine enemies: Thou anointest my head with oil; my cup runneth over.
> Surely goodness and mercy shall follow me all the days of my life: and I will dwell in the house of the Lord forever."
> (Psalm 23 KJV)

As my final moments approached, I called for Solomon and gave him these parting words:

"I am about to go the way of all the earth. Be strong and act like a man. Keep the commandments of the Lord your God, walk in His ways, and obey His decrees as written in the Law of Moses. If you do this, you will prosper, and the Lord will fulfill His promise to me that my descendants will rule Israel as long as they walk faithfully before Him." (1 Kings 2:2-4 paraphrased)

With a final blessing upon my son, I closed my eyes and began the journey through the valley of the shadow of death, comforted by the presence of my Shepherd. At last, I was ready to meet Him and my beloved infant child who had gone before me.

EPILOGUE

David passed away and was laid to rest with his ancestors in the City of David. He had reigned over Israel for forty years—seven years in Hebron and thirty-three in Jerusalem. Solomon, fulfilling David's final wishes, executed justice on Joab and Shimei for their past transgressions. In contrast, Solomon showed kindness to the sons of Barzillai of Gilead, in gratitude for their loyalty to David during his flight from Absalom.

David's Mighty Warriors

David's mighty warriors were renowned for their bravery and heroic feats.

Josheb-Basshebeth, a Tahkemonite, was the chief of the Three Mighty Warriors. He wielded his spear against eight hundred men, killing them in a single encounter.

Next was Eleazar, son of Dodai the Ahohite, one of the Three Mighty Warriors. He fought alongside David during a confrontation with the Philistines at Pas Dammim. When the Israelites retreated, Eleazar held his ground and fought until his hand was too weary to let go of his sword. That day, the Lord brought about a great victory. The troops returned, but only to strip the dead.

Another mighty warrior was Shammah, son of Agee the Hararite. When the Philistines gathered in a field of lentils and the Israelite troops fled, Shammah stood firm in the middle of the field, striking down the Philistines. Again, the Lord brought about a great victory.

During harvest time, the Three Mighty Warriors descended to join David in the cave of Adullam, while a band of Philistines encamped in the Valley of Rephaim. At that time, David was in a stronghold, with the Philistines garrisoned in Bethlehem. David longed for a drink of water from the well near the gate of Bethlehem and expressed his desire aloud. The Three Mighty Warriors broke through enemy lines, drew water from the well, and brought it back to him. However, David refused to drink it, instead pouring it out before the Lord. He said, "Far be it from me, Lord, to drink this water! It is the blood of men who risked their lives." So, he did not drink it.

Such were the deeds of the Three Mighty Warriors.

Other Notable Warriors

Abishai, the brother of Joab, son of Zeruiah, was chief of the Three. He raised his spear against three hundred men and killed them, becoming as famous as the Three. Although not officially one of the Three, he was honored above them and became their commander.

Benaiah, son of Jehoiada, a valiant warrior from Kabzeel, was also renowned for his exploits. He struck down Moab's two mightiest warriors, killed a lion in a pit on a snowy day, and defeated a formidable Egyptian by taking the Egyptian's own spear and killing him with it. Though not one of the Three, Benaiah was held in higher esteem than any of the Thirty and was placed in charge of David's personal bodyguard.

The Thirty Warriors

Among the Thirty were:
Asahel, the brother of Joab
Elhanan, son of Dodo from Bethlehem
Shammah the Harodite
Elika the Harodite
Helez the Paltite
Ira, son of Ikkesh from Tekoa
Abiezer from Anathoth
Sibbekai the Hushathite
Zalmon the Ahohite
Maharai the Netophathite
Heled, son of Baanah the Netophathite
Ithai, son of Ribai from Gibeah in Benjamin
Benaiah the Pirathonite
Hiddai from the ravines of Gaash
Abi-Albon the Arbathite
Azmaveth the Barhumite
Eliahba the Shaalbonite
The sons of Jashen
Jonathan, son of Shammah the Hararite
Ahiam, son of Sharar the Hararite

Eliphelet, son of Ahasbai the Maakathite
Eliam, son of Ahithophel the Gilonite
Hezro the Carmelite
Paarai the Arbite
Igal, son of Nathan from Zobah
The son of Hagri
Zelek the Ammonite
Naharai the Beerothite, armor-bearer of Joab, son of Zeruiah
Ira the Ithrite
Gareb the Ithrite
Uriah the Hittite, the husband of Bathsheba.
In total, there were thirty-seven mighty warriors.

David's Legacy Lives On:

The first verse of the New Testament lets us know that David's legacy lives on through Jesus Christ. Matthew 1:1 "The book of the generation of Jesus Christ, the Son of David, the Son of Abraham." (KJV)

We also see that Jesus' earthly father, Joseph, was from the lineage of David. Matthew 1:20 "But while he thought on these things, behold, the angel of the Lord appeared unto him in a dream, saying, 'Joseph, thou son of David, fear not to take unto thee Mary thy wife: for that which is conceived in her is of the Holy Ghost'." (KJV)

Jesus was called "Thou Son of David" numerous times by those that needed healing. Matthew records how Jesus challenged some Pharisees about who He was, using David as a reference. In Matthew 22:42-46 it says Jesus asked them: "Saying, 'what think ye of Christ? Whose Son is He?' 'They say unto Him, the Son of David.'

"He saith unto them, 'How then doth David in spirit call Him Lord, saying, The Lord said unto my Lord, Sit Thou on my right hand, till I make Thine enemies Thy footstool? If David then call Him Lord, how is He His Son?'

"And no man was able to answer Him a word, neither durst any man from that day forth ask Him any more questions." (KJV)

Jesus was trying to get them to understand that He was indeed the Messiah that David prophesied about in the Psalms.

Concerning the Messiah's birth:

The Messiah would come for all people (Psalm 18:49)

The Messiah would know His Father from childhood (Psalm 22:9)

The Messiah would be called by God while still in the womb (Psalm 22:10).

Concerning the Messiah's Nature and Name:

The Messiah would be called King of the Jews. (Psalm 2:6)

The Messiah would be the Son of God. (Psalm 2:7)

The Messiah would be Lord and King. (Psalm 110:1).

Concerning The Messiah's Ministry:

The Messiah would do God's (His Father's) will. (Psalm 40:7–8)

Political/religious leaders would conspire against the Messiah. (Psalm 2:1–3)

Concerning The Messiah's Betrayal and Death:

The Messiah would be despised and rejected by His own. (Psalm 22:6)

The Messiah would be mocked. (Psalm 22:7)

From the Messiah's body would flow blood and water. (Psalm 22:14)

The Messiah would be crucified. (Psalm 22:14)

The Messiah would thirst while dying. (Psalm 22:15)

The Messiah's hands and feet would be pierced. (Psalm 22:16)

The Messiah's garments would be parted among the soldiers through the casting of lots. (Psalm 22:18)

The Messiah would be accused by false witnesses. (Psalm 27:12)

The Messiah would cry out to God, "Into Thy hands I commend My Spirit." (Psalm 31:5)

The Messiah would have no bones broken. (Psalm 34:20)

The Messiah would be silent as a lamb before His accusers. (Psalm 38:13–14)

The Messiah would be God's sacrificial lamb for redemption of all mankind. (Psalm 40:6–8)

The Messiah would be betrayed by one of His own disciples. (Psalm 41:9)

The Messiah would be offered gall mingled with vinegar while dying. (Psalm 69:21)

Concerning The Messiah's Resurrection:

The Messiah would be resurrected. (Psalm 16:8–10)

The Messiah's body would not see corruption (natural decay) (Psalm 16:8–10)

The Messiah would ascend back into heaven. (Psalm 68:18)

David's name is mentioned in the first chapter of the New Testament (Matthew 1), and also in the last chapter of the New Testament (Revelation 22).

The only name mentioned in the Bible more than the name of David is the name of Jesus! (over 1,040 times). David's name is the only other name that even comes close to the name of Jesus. (over 990 times).

There is no question as to who is being referred to when someone uses the name "King David"!

His Kingdom endures forever:

In 2 Samuel 7:16 Nathan the prophet gave a word of prophecy to King David saying, "Your house and your kingdom will endure forever before Me; your throne will be established forever."

Jesus is our Eternal King who sits on the throne forever! And He can be the King and Lord of your life if you put your faith and trust in Him for your salvation. Do not wait, make the decision today to follow Him for the rest of your days.

THE END

FROM THE AUTHOR:

In my lifetime of growing up in a church I have seen numerous pastors and leaders fall to temptation. Most of these pastors and leaders were/are good people that, much like David, found themselves in a place where they fell to a temptation that was presented to them by the devil.

In no way am I seeking to justify sinful behavior, but I think all of us can say thank God for the mercy that was extended to David, not only by God, but also the people that surrounded David, resulting in some of the most heart rendering psalms and songs ever written.

King Solomon wrote in Proverbs 24 how a "righteous man falls seven times," yet he rises again.

Yes, it can be discouraging when a pastor or church leader falls to temptation, but Paul encourages us to restore those that have fallen.

Can I encourage you to pray for your pastor. Pray for your church staff and leaders. Pray for them to stand strong in these last evil days!

And if you know a pastor that has fallen to temptation but is trying to "rise the seventh time," come alongside him and be a source of encouragement and strength.

"...and lead us not into temptation but deliver us from all evil!

OTHER BOOKS BY THE AUTHOR:

The Adventures Of Matthew and Andy

(5 Book Series: Kids Books)

In this series of children's books, Matthew, a ten-year-old boy, has started reading his Bible but he is struggling to understand what he is reading. So, he prays and asks God to help him. God sends a very unique angel named Andy in Matthew's dreams to start taking him back in time to see first-hand how exciting the stories in the Bible can be.

Each Bible adventure is described with its exciting twists and turns as seen through the eyes of ten-year-old Matthew, with his quirky sidekick.

Bartholomew And The Christ Child

This fictitious story is about a fifteen-year-old boy named Bartholomew whose family owned the Bethlehem Inn, and how their encounter with Jesus as the Christ Child, born in their stable changed their lives.

The Five Marys

This story, while based on Biblical facts, is a fictitious story of the Mary's in Jesus' life, told from the viewpoint of Mary, the mother of Jesus. Each *Mary* saw Jesus perform numerous miracles, yet each one related to Jesus in different ways and have their own story to tell.